Love's Uncharted Path

by

David Dowson

www.daviddowson.com

Acknowledgements

Special thanks to my mother, Beryl, who is always there for me and my sister, Jan Webber, author of the *Betty Illustrated* Children's books.

Edition one

www.daviddowson.com
www.daviddowson.co.uk

Other books also written by David Dowson include:

Chess for Beginners
Chess for Beginners Edition 2
Into the Realm of Chess Calculation
Nursery Rhymes
The Path of a Chess Amateur

BEGINNERS GUIDE eBook: Declon Five.

Dangers within
The murder of Inspector Hine

TABLE OF CONTENTS

CHAPTER ONE

Sarah Reed was a typical girl, at least in her opinion. She did whatever it took to stay out of trouble, especially when it involved boys. She believed they were nothing but trouble and stayed clear of them no matter what anybody told her.

Boys, they always mess things up without even realizing it. She was finicky about things like that because sometimes boys do not use common sense. Many people would have called her a lady who overreacted, but she didn't mind. They hadn't been through what she had, so she wasn't a fan of going into details. She just wanted to stew in her dislike and hope that no man was crazy enough to come within ten feet of her. She didn't think she was being unreasonable in how she acted because most men only wanted to play around, with no thought of commitment. It made her stand firmly on her previous notions that having anything to do with men for a long time would be nothing short of heartache and depression. There were no two ways about it. She preferred to be alone; there was less drama, and she didn't have to babysit anyone.

The way opened before her, and she inhaled, taking a massive dose of the morning breeze. She liked nature. Nature was straightforward and didn't try to stab her in the back. Nature was understandable, even with the whole natural disasters thing going on. That was easy to wrap her head around, but men went a different breed entirely. She had a lot of stored-up resentments for the men, and who could blame her? Her last relationship didn't go so well. She didn't like to think about it because she got cranky and irritated whenever she did.

Men do not love. Not always.

Sometimes, she wondered if things would have gone differently had she slowed down and understood the intricacies associated with the minds of the men. Maybe she wouldn't have been thrown under the bus so cruelly if only she had anticipated such betrayal.

"Let it go, Sarah. Que Sera, Sera. Whatever would be, would be," That's what her best friend usually told her, but how could she?

A lot had happened, a lot that took so much from her. Even if she were on the forgiveness train, seeing a man as dependable or even reachable would take a long time. Sure, they were always around whenever they needed something, but as soon as they got it, they usually hightailed it out of there. She supposed it was in their DNA, the way they acted. There is no sense of responsibility, just living life each day as it comes and breaking hearts while at it.

I'll never leave you, I promise. I won't budge. You're mine. I'm all yours.

All lies she'd heard before. He promised, didn't he? But what did it matter? Promises were meant to be broken, as they say. That's why he had no qualms about leaving and didn't even wonder what would happen to her if he left. He just up and left, no questions asked.

You're the only one for me, and I can't imagine living with anyone else.

Lies. All lies from the pit of hell. She wondered how many girls he must have said that too if she was just one of his easy marks, scammed of affection. She felt stupid, the biggest idiot of all. Her only crime was falling in love. Why was it so hard to do something as simple as that? Why? It wasn't meant to stress her or make her wonder if she'd failed. It was meant to build her as a person, but the disgrace his leaving brought, she wouldn't have wished it on anyone else, even the guy in question.

While walking, she bumped into something solid and raised her head to see what it was. She stared into the startling blue eyes of a human wall as if the wall chose to be sexy as sin with the body of an Adonis.

"Hi, preoccupied much?" He opened his mouth to speak, and she felt weak-kneed. His husky voice seemed to put her into a daze, but she shook it off almost immediately. She wasn't an easy mark, she wasn't a mark at all, and the sooner the men got that, the better for everyone else because she was tired of being treated like a senseless doll, as though all she had going for her was her beauty and being a woman. She needed that stereotype to end.

"Sorry." She said and moved out of his way, not bothering to look up at him again. She steered clear of men like that; they were the world's fundamental problems, and they didn't even know it yet. Most of them usually leave a trail of heartbroken women in their wake like it's no big deal, and sometimes she wondered if that was the kind of life they were satisfied with. Knowing them, they didn't overthink their actions or how many people it affected. As long as they could have fun, they didn't care.

"Don't leave." He called out, but she rolled her eyes, moving forward. She didn't need to return to know he was still waiting for her. It was one of their famous antics, and it worked with some women, but she was not *some* women. She was Sarah Reed and would do whatever it took to ensure she didn't go through the whole heartbreak situation again.

Some would call her callous for judging a book by its cover but it was better safe than sorry. She didn't remotely think of giving anyone else a chance because she could see it in their eyes, hear it in their voices. They all felt they were too irresistible, too powerful. Like some mafia lord in a fictional novel. But real life wasn't fiction and she blamed some women for treating those men like they were the best things to come out of the earth.

It inflated their egos to dangerous levels and sometimes she wondered what would happen once a man's ego hit its limits. She was curious but not stupid enough to see how that would play out. There was a difference between being curious and acting on it. Sometimes acting on curiosity leads to unintended consequences. But was it really unintended? If it was clear that the situation wasn't a favourable one and you kept poking the hole, all in the name of curiosity. Sarah was many things but stupidity was far from her.

"You should calm down, you know. Get a feel of the air. Understand yourself deeply. It's time to do some soul searching, time to find out what's missing and deal with

whatever comes your way." Sarah's long-term best friend advised, staring at her friend in silence, worry creasing her forehead. They were in a diner but Sarah had barely touched her food. There was no reason to prod her anyways because the food had gone cold.

"Don't worry about me, I'm doing just great. How are you, h?" Sarah asked, turning the question back at her friend and Renee recognized the tactic, she used it sometimes when she wanted to get out of an unpleasant conversation or an uncomfortable one. It worked wonders, especially if you knew the right things to say.

"I'm great. I just worry about you, you know? How long has it been?" Sarah didn't need to ask what Renee was referring to, it was a moment in time that she couldn't forget, no matter how hard she tried. It haunted her, worse than anything else in the world.

"Three years, five months, and twelve days." Sarah replied, not bothering to calculate it because it was ingrained into her soul, the moment she realized how cruel life could be.

"Not every man is like that, you know? You have to give someone else a chance. Please. He was a deadbeat, he treated you in a way you didn't deserve and I'm sorry about that. But you're stronger than this, aren't you? You can find your way through

this. It's gone on for too long and I want you to know I'm solidly behind you but you need to trust yourself too. You need to let go of the restraints, please." Renee said, placing a hand on Sarah's hand, eyes staring at each other, a silent pact of solidarity formed between the two women.

"Thank you, Renee. For always looking out for me. You suggested we move in together when the whole ordeal happened and that's one of the best decisions I've ever made. I'm grateful." Sarah said with a smile as sincere as she could make it.

"Don't mention it; what are friends for? Also, I might eat your pie." Renee said, eyeing the cold and untouched pie just sitting dejectedly in front of Sarah.

"You can have it, I'm done anyway. I should go grocery shopping. We need some supplies. You can go on ahead of me to the house. It's a weekend, rest a little. You don't have to work so hard." She lightly chided her best friend and Renee had a look of mock seriousness when she replied, "Yes ma'am!"

Sarah was content with her friendship and even though she didn't give Renee a straight answer to avoid breaking her friend's heart, she knew deep down that her heart was closed to men and their shenanigans. They could as well tap dance in front of her if they wanted and not a single thing would change. She didn't like them and she wasn't ever really going to. They were just a set of people she avoided, especially when they tried to make small talk at the office or show off for her. It was childish but she wasn't truly surprised. She knew that men never grew up, not where it mattered.

She loved working, but only if one man or the other wasn't trying to bug her. The women at work knew of her situation so, they protected her whenever the men tried to come too close or act too friendly. She was grateful she had a sort of sisterhood that could take care of things for her if push came to shove. The craziest part is none of them really talked about it, they just decided unanimously, without saying a word. That's another thing the men didn't share because the size of their egos didn't allow them to think outside the box, to abase themselves so they'd understand.

"Hello, good morning Sarah," an elderly old woman she frequently visited called out to her from the other side of the road and she waved merrily.

"Good morning to you too, Mrs. Dodds. I'll be coming over later, please make time for me." She said a decibel higher than intended and Mrs. Dodds just smiled and nodded as she was wheeled away. Sarah had known her for a long time, and Mrs. Dodds was one of the women she looked up to. Resilient even after a divorce that took almost everything out of her. After 30 years of marriage. It was something Sarah couldn't wrap her head around, but she had to, for the older woman's sake. That was another thing that cemented her convictions that men weren't meant to live amongst normal people, not when they acted like animals. *Let's get this over with.*

She walked into the supermarket just a stone throw from where she met Mrs. Dodds, wondering if she'd meet the handsome guy again and put him down so bad, he'd go back home and rethink his life choices. Sure, she was the one who bumped into him but he didn't need to flirt in that situation, not only was it unseemly, it was a level of arrogance bordering on narcissism. She couldn't tolerate narcissism, it always rubbed her wrong. It was the result of an ego inflated to bursting, she supposed. A self inflated ego on most cases. She slowed down as soon as she got to the supermarket door and silently ran over what she wanted to buy in her head. As she was still trying to piece everything together, she heard a voice behind her.

"Hello, you ran away." It was a voice she recognized too well, even though she'd only heard it once. A voice that had the arrogance she hated, a voice that seemed so self-assured, she was tempted to deflate the ego that was roaring like a volcano for all to see. She turned and standing behind her was Mr. Pretty, or was it Handsome? She wasn't that good with giving nicknames.

"Hi, I came to get some stuff from the supermarket too," he said, explaining things she never asked of him. It was weird and she didn't want to be in that situation anymore so, she didn't honor him with a reply, just walked into the supermarket as the door swiveled and left him on the other side.

His rightful place.

CHAPTER TWO

Sarah had never seen a man who was so… insufferably beautiful. His eyes, his full lips. Even from the other side of the transparent door, she was sure that he was trouble with a capital T. He looked it anyways. And she shook her head a few times to get the image of him out of there because she couldn't make sense of things if thoughts of him were hovering over her. He could scramble her brain without a word ad those were the kind of men she took extra care to steer clear of. Because everything was a game to them, especially hearts. They didn't care, they didn't know how to. They just found whatever woman that catches their fancy for the week and go ahead to turn their charm on her. It worked; mostly. But not to someone like her, never.

She slowed down her racing heart, and walked into the vast supermarket, silently cursing herself for forgetting everything she wanted to buy. She knew that she should have written it somewhere but she didn't, and that was the problem. If she'd done that, she could have used it as a reference but her memory was something she was proud of, something that hadn't failed her. Until now. *He's trouble and no matter what, I can't let him get too close, or even close at all.* She silently steeled her resolve and decided to take the shopping step by step because if she was being honest, it felt better that way, saner too. And she could make sense of her emotions, whatever they were. She needed to clear her head because if she was being honest, she couldn't go through with life disoriented. She was the kind of person who loved things being orderly and would do whatever it takes to ensure they stay that way. A lot of people would have called her an orderly freak but that was the only way she could process all the information the world was sending her way. *I can't afford to make a mistake. I can't afford to let down my guard.*

She'd lived that way ever since she dropped her carefree attitude, when life showed her that there were different facets to it and she couldn't afford to be lax. That was what got her in trouble in the first place.

"You don't have to look so lost, I don't bite you know." She heard a voice just behind her and turning to look behind her, she found him. Reclining on the wall, staring at her. He had an intensity to him, the earlier playfulness lost in his facial features. He seemed more mature for some reason.

"Why are you following me?" She asked him, careful to phrase her words well. She didn't think he was a threat, not really. He was just being friendly when she didn't want to be associated with that sort of friendship. She wanted to be by herself, and for good reason.

"Sorry, am I making you uncomfortable? If I am, I apologize. I'm new here. Or maybe new isn't the word. I've been here before, but that was many years ago. Moved overseas and studied. Just returned a week ago and well, this town doesn't seem to have much going on. A quaint little town, as expected. So, you were a bright spot in my day. I definitely didn't mean to get you running with your tails between your legs." She wasn't sure what he was trying to do, provoke her or apologize. He seemed to be trying to do both.

"You didn't send me running, not with my tail between my legs. I don't really talk to strangers. You seem nice enough but... I'm just not interested in a friendship for now." She knew that she must have sounded harsh but she couldn't sugarcoat things, that wasn't the way she worked and if he didn't like it, he could as well leave her alone as she intended. It was the same with killing two birds with one stone. She'd get him to leave her alone and she'd also bruise his ego. As she intended. But it didn't work just as she planned. Not in the least. He stared at her for a few seconds and burst out laughing.

"Why are you laughing?" She asked, suddenly peeved. She thought he was making fun of her, which was the complete reverse of how it was supposed to go. He was the one who was meant to slink away, with shame and frustration at the very least.

"Oh, I'm not laughing at you, Nah. It's just refreshing to see someone as feisty as you. Makes me feel like my trip here wasn't a waste."

Her blood ran cold immediately as a memory jumped at her out of the blue; a memory she would have done anything to forget, to throw into the deepest part of the nether.

"I love you; especially with how feisty you are. I don't think there's anyone else that can do the things you do." He said to her, two weeks before leaving. Two weeks. It wasn't even a month.

"Goodbye." She said to the new guy that she didn't even get his name, neither did she care to. The word feisty annoyed her to no end. Because her ex was fond of using it, especially when she got ticked off by something or someone. He was once her safe space and then, he just left.

"What did I do? I'm sorry!" The new guy called out but she didn't stop, even if she'd only bought half of what she originally intended to buy. She needed to be out of there fast, her mind was reeling and she was suddenly feeling claustrophobic even in the open space. She got to the cashier and paid, not looking back to see if the new guy was following her. She was out the door like a light, finding her way back home before anything else.*It was a mistake to walk. But then; I wouldn't have been able to drive like this.*The open air helped, as her claustrophobia died down and she felt... calm. It was therapeutic, and she wondered what she must have looked like to the new guy. It was probably best if they went their separate ways because she wasn't really sure what he needed from her. For one, he wasn't annoyed by the way she talked to him, blew it away like it was nothing. Secondly, he laughed. And his laugh was beautiful, she could admit that much to herself. He showed perfect dentition and she wondered just how many women would have swooned just from that. It was clear he had a healthy self-esteem but she couldn't be sure if it was healthy or narcissism too far gone. There was sometimes no visible distinction between the two of them. As soon as she got home, she poured water on her face, staring into the mirror and giving herself a little pep talk.*You're stronger than this, Sarah. You can't let any Tom, Dick or Harry mess with your mental health. You're strong, you need to show them that. Don't falter, don't fall.*

"Sarah? Are you in there?" Renee called out and Sarah realized that she never told Renee she was back, just made her way to the bathroom like hell itself was on her tail.

"Y-yes, I'm here." She said, willing her voice to stop shaking so much. She needed to present a bold front to Renee even though it was almost impossible to hide anything from her.

"Are you fine? What's wrong?" Renee asked from the other side of the door and Sarah closed her eyes, wondering what she was going to say. She didn't want to worry Renee but if she took too long to answer, that would be even worse. And if her voice was shaky, that was going to be a red flag.

She needed the perfect distraction. So, she took a toothbrush and began to brush her teeth.

"Oh, you're just brushing your teeth. That's fine, I'm in the kitchen, call me if you need anything." Renee said and her voice faded as her footfalls echoed down the hallway. Sarah heaved a sigh of relief. She couldn't blame Renee for checking up on her though, she was a complete mess the first two years after the unfortunate incident that happened to her. And Renee stood by her, thicker than glue. She was sure that nobody could ever replace what she had for Renee. The love and camaraderie between them. They were beyond best friends, they were family. Which was precisely why she couldn't heap so much pressure on Renee. Renee already had a lot going on and Sarah needed to stand on her own two feet.

"I'm sorry, Renee. Sorry for having you take care of me always." Sarah said to her reflection in the mirror, her tone sombre. She washed her mouth with water and went out of the bathroom to look for Renee. She was standing in the kitchen, cataloguing the stuff Sarah bought.

"Eggs, milk; more milk? That's weird. Toiletries, check. And chicken? Maybe we'd need that. Hmmm, weird. There are a lot of things written that aren't here. Maybe a mistake?" Sarah listened to Renee's monologue and felt instantly guilty because they had an unspoken agreement that whoever was going to the supermarket would get whatever was needed for the entire week.

"Sorry, I couldn't get everything. Something came up." Sarah said, resigned to fate. She couldn't avoid it anymore and Renee was her best friend, she was definitely going to understand.

"Talk to me. What happened?" Renee asked, her forehead creased with worry. The exact thing Sarah was trying to avoid. She felt bad all of a sudden. But Renee deserved the truth, so Sarah told her everything.

"Did he try to touch you? Say something!" Renee was beside herself in anger and Sarah wondered if she didn't pass the right information across.

"No, no, no, nothing like that," she hurriedly said, scared that Renee would take the cause upon her and wreak havoc unlike never before seen.

"What then?" Renee asked, her body poised for a fight. She looked like she was positively able to murder someone

"Nothing. That's the thing. He wasn't rude, neither did he act like a douchebag. Honestly, he was a perfect gentleman. It's just... the word triggered me..." Sarah tried to explain and trailed off lamely, realizing how utterly childish she sounded. Which was not her intention but it happened anyway.

"I understand perfectly. He triggered your PTSD. I'm sorry this happened to you. We need to take great care to make sure you don't see him anymore. But before then, come give me a hug. You look like you need it." Renee opened her arms and Sarah rushed inside, feeling safe for the first time since she returned from the store. She was home, she was safe and whatever was going to happen after, she was safe in the knowledge that with Renee, she could be herself. The next day, she decided to take it slow and Renee woke up before her. It was a work day, so she was strangely looking forward to it. Which was weird because she wasn't always a fan of work. But after the events of the past day, she wanted to put everything behind her and have a fresh start.

"Would you be fine?" Renee asked as she prepared and Sarah nodded in the affirmative, knowing deeply that whatever was going to come, she was equipped to handle it and not break a sweat. Because that was just the kind of person she was.

"Yes. I have a good feeling about today." Sarah replied and Renee smiled back. They had a healthy relationship and could talk about everything. That was what made their bond even tighter. The fact that their vulnerability with each other wasn't a problem, it was a blessing.

"I believe in you, you know that, right?" Renee asked after a while and Sarah walked up to her and gave her a hug.

"That, was for helping me when I was breaking apart yesterday. And this," Sarah said, pulling lightly on Renee's cheeks, "is for everything else. I believe in you too, silly. You're my best friend in the whole world."

"You mean your only friend. I'm your only friend." Renee corrected and Sarah burst out laughing. Then she said in mock consternation, "Now that you know my secret, I'll eat you up." Renee just rolled her eyes.

"You can't even hurt a fly. Even a dead one."

"Can't you see those things? They're so helpless and I can't bring myself to hurt them." Sarah said, giving Renee the puppy dog eyes. It usually worked, sometimes.

"That just buttresses my point. Doesn't it? Have fun today, Sarah. And tell me all about it as soon as you get home. Promise?" Sarah nodded in the affirmative. They both hugged and left for work in their cars. Sarah got to work in a good mood, whistling even. She greeted most of her coworkers and they in turn greeted her too. Things were looking up, and the past day was just a misstep on her part, a mistake. Nothing more, nothing less. And she was going to get a fresh start. Until she heard a voice from behind her, again. A voice she'd have recognized anywhere in the world.

"Hi. You're here."

And of course, the pretty boy was behind her, a smile on his face. The day had just gotten a thousand times worse.

CHAPTER THREE

She didn't know exactly what to do or how to react to what she was currently seeing. She thought it was a prank or maybe she was dreaming but he was just standing there, a pleasant smile on his face. If it was a knowing smirk, that would have been expected. But the smile was so sweet, it made her heart ache. She hated herself for that.

"What are you doing here?" She said, laying emphasis on every single word. Her eyes burning with barely restrained fury. She couldn't believe he was stalking her. It was the most despicable thing to do.

"I work here. That's why I moved in the first place." He explained but she wasn't having it. What were the odds of such a thing happening? Low was an understatement.

"If I find out you've been stalking me, I'd file a restraining order against you. Good day." She said and walked away after dropping that scathing remark. She didn't know how she was going to see her workplace anymore, with all of the things going on around her. She wanted to crawl into a place and just be for a while, undisturbed and away from the madness all around her. She was still fuming later that day, and everybody did well to stay out of her way because it was clear that whoever stood in her path was going to get a stern talking to, no matter who it was. She heard a few of the guys talking in hushed tones to each other, asking if it was her time of the month. She didn't really care, they could talk, as long as they didn't talk to her. That was where she drew the line. Then suddenly, an emergency meeting was called and she felt... off. She wondered if she was the reason but it didn't add up, even as she thought about it, it made no sense that they'd call a meeting just because of her. The CEO was in attendance, which made it all the more official since he was a 60-something-year-old man and he wasn't ever really seen.

"Good, you're all here. The reason I called this meeting is to introduce the new manager. The one that we've been trying to get our hands on for over three years, my son. He's absolutely brilliant and due to a stroke of luck, he decided to move here.

Permanently. Having handled a lot of businesses in the past, he's what most people would call a business tycoon and from today, he's your new boss. He only answers to me, and that's on occasions. Welcome the future of Harding Company, Jacob Harding."

And then it clicked. He was being sincere when he told her he wasn't there for her and she overreacted, to the one person who could get her fired. Not only that, she disrespected him in front of everyone, without knowing who he was. But, she wasn't bothered about it, she didn't mind being fired either. Her credentials were good and she was sure to find a job even if she was fired. She blamed him for letting her get the wrong idea because if he'd been honest with her from the start, she'd have known just what a big shot he was and would have acted accordingly. Or maybe she wouldn't have, because she wasn't a fan of being made fun of, even if it was a harmless little prank. She looked his way and saw him staring at her, and then he winked. She was beyond livid by then, wondering if he thought that little of her or if he just wanted to mess with her. With the way he'd been acting, it was probably both. Which did nothing to endear him towards her. In fact, she wanted to rant and rave but she was in the workplace and would be there for an hour more at the very least. That irked her to no end. After the CEO left, her other coworkers surrounded Jacob and were talking about how pleased they were to have him. It was the typical ass-kissing that they did whenever someone was a rank or two above them. And she hated it. It was clear they were all sycophants, and she wanted nothing to do with their way of life. As soon as it was time to leave, she knew she'd be out the door before anybody else. In the meantime, she put her head down and focused on the job she was there to do.

That was all she could do anyway. The drive home was a sombre one. One that made her feel so many things at the same time. She turned on the music but it felt too loud, too intrusive, so she turned it off. The silence in the car started to feel deafening, so she winded down a little and let the sounds around her sink into her soul. She wasn't angry, angry was a baby word. She was exasperated, livid, knackered and frustrated beyond measure. In fact, she wanted to hit something, anything. But there was nothing in sight, short of her dashboard. And she didn't want to hit *that*, she loved her car. Didn't want to risk anything happening to it in blind rage. It was clear Jacob or whatever his name was, was toying with her. Over and over again, without fail. He was doing it as though he didn't take note of it, but she knew the truth. He was doing it to get to her, and *boy*, did he get to her. He got on her nerves in so many ways, it would have been downright comical if there was humour to be seen in the situation. She wondered if this was payback in some sort of way even if she didn't know what exactly she did to deserve it. Jacob wasn't a bad guy, not really. But he was someone she needed to avoid because all their meetings proved that he wasn't good for her sanity, not in the long run anyway. He was too unpredictable and no matter how handsome or how skilful he was, she decided that staying clear of him would do the both of them a world of good.

If only he wasn't her boss. The entire situation was something out of a romantic's daydream and her worst nightmares. She wasn't a romantic, she left it for those who could handle heartache and whatever else romance brought with it. It was a full package, and for the first three months, only one side of the entire thing was seen. She wasn't going to be deceived anymore, not while she knew how people worked and what went on in their minds. People would call her cynical and they wouldn't be wrong, she was cynical but it wasn't for a bad reason, not really. She had every right to be. And the men met were nothing short of obnoxious, fueling her previous assumption. It was clear that love wasn't in the cards for her, even if some supreme being manipulated the outcome. She was going to fight tooth and nail against it. She wasn't going to be caged by a concept anymore. Not while she still drew breath. She parked in front of her house and turned off the engine of her car. Took a few deep breaths and came out, hoping that Renee was around. She wasn't. And so for the next hour, Sarah only had herself for company. And if she was being honest, she was the wrong sort of company. The memories hung at the edge of her vision, threatening to pull her under. This time, she let them. *It was a sunny day and then, the clouds suddenly converged, darkening the sky.*

"Here, have my jacket. It's about to rain. Race you to that bench over there?" He said, pointing to a bench under a shade on the other side of the road. She grinned. That was her kind of game.

"You're so on. Don't come crying to me when I whoop your ass." She said and he chuckled, then ran.

"Wait, that's cheating!" She called out, running after him. They were both laughing by the time they got to the other side, mere seconds from the bench. And then, the rain came pouring down. He covered her with his body and she could smell his aftershave, the pure masculinity in his powerfully built body.

"I'll protect you, even from the rain." He said, his voice a tad huskier than it was a few moments before. She looked up at him and swallowed, his eyes darkening. They were startling green, usually. Like blades of grass. But staring at him at that moment, she couldn't be sure what the colours of his eyes were. It was as though she was staring at a kaleidoscope, and the colours were too deep for her feeble mind to

decipher. He was magic. And he was hers. She hated that memory and if she could burn it, she would have. It was the memory of a man who would shake the world to its foundations to see her safe, a man who was hers, at one point in time. The pain lancing through her body was no child's play, she could feel the outpouring of emotions, her body shaking from the intensity of it. *Why did I have to fall in love with you?*

She asked herself that question many times in a single day and no answer was forthcoming. She wasn't sure there was really an answer to that question and that was what made it infinitely worse. She couldn't forget, no matter how she tried. It was as though she'd been branded by a rod of steel dipped in magma. There was a constant reminder, one she couldn't run away from, no matter how she tried. It haunted her every waking moment. That was the price she was paying for loving someone, the ultimate price that nothing could ever take away from her. It was life. And she wasn't liking it one bit. Renee's return made Sarah so happy because she could at least tiptoe around her memories, distract herself and let them simmer down. Because she wasn't sure she could confront those memories without tearing up. No matter how angry she was, the memories were at her core, her most vulnerable. The one place she couldn't hide, couldn't run away from. It was irksome on most days. "So, you're telling me he's your new boss?" Renee asked as soon as Sarah had given her all the details. She was barely through the door when Sarah accosted her with details of what transpired at her workplace and Renee was a good listener as always, she dropped her bag on the chair and listened to Sarah without saying a word. That was also one of the most enviable things about her.

"Yes. He is. My new boss; can't believe I'm saying this out loud. It's funny but it's also not. I just don't know anymore. He wasn't stalking me, not really. And he was new. Everything he said was true. That doesn't make it better though." Sarah admitted, much to herself than to Renee.

"I understand." Renee said and Sarah was grateful for that. Renee didn't force her to talk or try to get into her head or even heap blames on her head even though she was clearly at fault. Renee was letting Sarah work things out herself and that was admirable, at least in Sarah's opinion.

"Thank you for being with me." Sarah said out of the blue and Renee pulled her into a hug. "Have you forgotten that I'm your only friend? I have to watch over you. You're like my little baby." Renee said, squeezing Sarah's cheeks fondly.

"You're not even older than me." Sarah pointed out and Renee held a hand out.

Six days count for something. I was alive for six whole days before you were born. I'm definitely your senior." It was a running gag between the two of them, especially when they wanted to make light of a situation. Renee had been her friend since college and they were thick as thieves. In fact, they'd been inseparable ever since they met. It was friendship at first sight.

"I don't know what to do about him through. But I definitely don't want to apologize. He gave mixed signals and he can as well suffer for it." Sarah said, knowing that she was acting stubborn but she didn't care. If he wanted to be that way, then two can play that game.

"That's my girl." Renee said and Sasha raised an eyebrow in query.

"You're not going to stop me or tell me that I'm doing the wrong thing?" She asked and Renee waved it away.

"Nope. Never. I trust you to make the best decisions for you. And if he's being this way, he needs to be taught a lesson. That's all there is to it." Renee explained.

"I love you." Sarah said, sincerity shining in her eyes.

"I love you too, girl. Raise hell." Renee said, a wicked smirk playing on her face.

"Do you remember who you're talking to?" Sarah said, rhetorically.

"Of course, just checking. Give me all the details." Renee responded and Sarah promised to do just that. They were thick as thieves anyway. And the way they showed love wasn't the way other people did and that was okay, because they weren't other people. They were vulnerable and talked about their issues before it escalated. They were perfect and when two perfect people schemed... God help the world.

CHAPTER FOUR

Jacob didn't know what to do with himself. He liked Sarah, he got her name from one of his subordinates. She was fiery, displaying the kind of emotions that only a redhead could. He loved it for her, even if she reacted to him like he was a plague or something. He wasn't used to that, at all. When he first graduated from Cambridge, women were all over him. He couldn't focus on his masters. So, he put it aside for a while and just let the entire thing wash over him. He decided to handle a few businesses while at it and found out he had a knack for multiplying money and expanding businesses. In two years, he'd turned a small-time company into one of the most sought-after companies in the world. Then, he became a consultant for small businesses seeking to expand. He bought shares and helped the companies grow. People began to call him a business prodigy. But he didn't really care about such names, they were just tags. He didn't care. There was just something about numbers that excited him. He could practically feel them leap off a page and welcome him like a long-lost friend. They listened to him, they did his bidding. He wasn't sure what that was that was called but calling it a talent seemed farfetched. He knew what the numbers were thinking, how they'd react to an opposition. They were like clay in his hands and he could mould them as he saw fit. But no, they were friends, his friends. But people didn't understand that, so he didn't bother explaining. He really wanted to be friends with Sarah though, temper and all. She didn't remind him of anyone if he was being honest, people mostly tried to suck up to him. She didn't care. Which was best because if she did, she'd have become one of the other women in his life hogging him for attention. After three to four years of helping businesses grow, he decided to do his masters once and for all. And he aced it. Then, he decided to return to his roots. Which was how he met Sarah.He knew that she wasn't going to believe that it was pure coincidence, seeing her way into him was nothing short of comedic and he laughed for a long time that day after she left in a hurry. She was intriguing, in more ways than one. She made him want to try things he hadn't tried before, made him want to do things, experience things. He wasn't used to such sensations, it felt completely alien to him. He wanted to explore the sensations but she wasn't even giving him a chance to explain himself. It'd been a week since he assumed the role of manager but she hadn't so much as exchanged a single word with him while the others tried to talk him to death, asking about totally irrelevant things. He answered graciously though, he was used to being the centre of attention, he just wasn't used to being blatantly ignored like a piece of furniture. It was intriguing. He tried to talk to her but she just acted like he didn't exist. He took extra care perusing her projects and she was one of the best at what she did. Even though he'd seen a lot of people in action, she stood out. It wasn't as though she was doing what hadn't been done before, not really. What stood out was the way she did it. She was unorthodox and absolutely brilliant. He loved it for her. If only she could give him a chance. One single chance. Life was funny like that, the one he genuinely wanted to talk to, didn't want to have anything to do with him. He supposed it was a sense of poetic justice, the irony of life in all its many forms. And somehow, it was glorious. He wanted to befriend her but she wasn't sure how to go about befriending someone who didn't even want to see his face, someone who would rather he dropped off the face of the earth. He wasn't sure how to deal with that. Or even if he could.

That was another challenge and he loved challenges.

"Mr. Hardings, sir? What would you like me to get you?" He turned to look at who spoke and it was a girl who'd appointed herself as his receptionist or personal assistant or whatever. She was good-looking, yes. But he'd had enough of good-looking people to last a lifetime. And she was making it clear that she wanted him and the whole job situation was just a way to get to him. Usually, they'd have annoyed him but he'd dealt with her sort for so long, it wasn't really a bother.

"Nothing, for now, Diane. Thank you." He said in his best professional voice, making it clear that he wanted nothing to do with her in the most polite way possible. Although he also knew that even if she got that, she wasn't going to adhere to it. There were so many of them like that, it was dizzying. But giving them attention was what made them come back even stronger and he wasn't ready to deal with such resilience. He acted as though he was busy and after seeing him like that, her common sense took over and she bowed and left the room. He heaved a sigh of relief. If he was being honest, he would rather wrestle a bear than deal with whatever shenanigans she concocted out of thin air. He liked his life simple and most people tried to complicate it by projecting their wants on him without even asking what he wanted. It was something he learnt to get used to, because he was always in the public's eye. No matter how much he tried.

It was funny how such a big company like his father's was in a small town but it was one of the branches. His father favoured large businesses. He only made a big deal out of Jacob's arrival in the company because his son was one of the most elite businessmen in the world and one of the most eligible bachelors. It was all a drag. Tiring too. He stared outside the window of the sky rise, overlooking a beautiful sunset. Night in a small town was refreshing, it made all his worries flow into a spot in time where they had no hold over him anymore. And he was going to try again the next day; and the day after that. Because life itself was a challenge and he loved challenges. It'd been three weeks since he assumed his role as manager and still, Sarah wasn't talking to him. It would have been comical if he wasn't getting worried. Sure, if he asked her to explain something, she did without much prompting. But aside from work, they were practically alienated from each other and that worried him more than he liked to say because she was intriguing, she was fun and he wanted to get to know her more. Although it was pretty much impossible. She was completely closed off to him and he didn't know what it was that he did wrong. Or maybe she just didn't like him, which would explain a lot because if he was being honest, he didn't think that there was anything he could say or do that would assuage whatever it was she felt. And even if he wanted to apologize, what was he supposed to be apologizing for? It sounded phoney even to him. So, he contented himself with just watching and hoping she'd come around. At least that's what was supposed to happen but it didn't. She didn't come around, she didn't even act like she was ever going to. Diane kept throwing herself at him in reckless abandon and he wondered what new ways he had to employ to keep her at bay because if he was being honest with himself, he was getting tired of her antics. And she didn't seem like she was going to stop anytime soon. Just his rotten luck. He mostly frequented the supermarket where Sarah walked out on him the first time, hoping to catch a glimpse of her and who would blame him? She was pretty exciting and he wanted to be the one she looked at as a friend. He wasn't sure he wanted more than that but he couldn't tell because she didn't bother to find out what kind of person he was.Strangely, that hurt. He didn't think of himself as threatening, even though he was fit and built pretty well. But he did all that to keep in shape, nothing more. He'd never tried to intimidate anyone with his body, not while he had a thousand and one things to be doing. It just didn't make sense for him to put so much time into acting like a total idiot. It wasn't his style. He preferred the direct approach, not cutting through corners. That was for people who weren't confident in themselves. He had a healthy dose of confidence, he could say as much. He didn't try to put people down and tried his best to understand the viewpoints of other people. So, he couldn't really see a reason why Sarah didn't want to talk to him.

After a month passed and she didn't make any effort to bridge the gap, he decided to do it himself. And of course, it was in the supermarket. He was there to grab a few things when she entered, looking around as though wary of something. He wondered what it was. It was a scary thought to imagine her being pursued.

"Hi. You're here." She was the one who spoke this time, arms akimbo. He didn't even know when she made her way to him, he wasn't paying attention so it skipped him completely. He was shocked to see her in front of him if he was being honest. But he steeled himself. She wasn't going to unnerve him, never.

"Hi to you too. I thought you didn't want to talk to me?" He said, not turning to look at her. He could see her pretty well from his side eye but he didn't give her the satisfaction of him turning to look at her. Which probably grated on her nerves.

"I don't. I just want to know what you want from me." She said, and he heard her voice break. He felt... pain. He didn't realize that the person she was wary of; was him.

"I'm sorry. I won't come here again. For what it's worth, I think you're a cool person and I wanted to be friends. But I came off as creepy and I apologize. I can't change jobs, not after my word to the board of directors but I'd do my best to stay out of your way. Good day." He nodded and went his way, not bothering to look behind him.

It did hurt to know that someone was scared of him, someone he wanted to befriend. He began to analyze her actions and he could see where he began to come off as creepy. A day after he followed her to the supermarket, he appeared at her workplace under a bogus claim. Of course, she'd feel insecure. He wanted to slap himself but he held back. He paid the cashier with his card and was out the door knowing that he wasn't going to go back to that supermarket. Ever. It didn't matter anymore.

"Hi." He heard her voice from behind him and hoped his ears weren't playing tricks on him. He was almost at his car door. A sleek convertible.

"Hi." He said tentatively as she stood a few feet in front of him, blushing visibly.

"I'm sorry." She said and he shook his head, hoping his ears were functioning tightly.

"What?" He asked, merely to be sure.

"I'm sorry," she said again and took a deep breath. "I took you for someone you were not and created a mental narrative of you, one you weren't aware of. I guess I've been rude and unkind to you. I'm sorry about that. The entire thing smelled fishy but I've done my research and I'm sorry for laying such heavy allegations on you." She said and he was at a loss for words. Even when apologizing, she was radiant. He wondered if he'd ever seen someone like her before.

"I just understood what was going on today. You thought I was stalking you, didn't you? I'm so sorry about that. I've been so obtuse. I didn't even realize. I was just excited to see a face I could recognize amidst all the new ones." He hoped that he was able to explain himself to her in the best way possible because honestly, there was nothing he could do anymore.

“Can we start over? The proper way?” He asked and she nodded in the affirmative, and he smiled, a genuine smile from the heart. They shook on it and decided to stay in touch. That moment lingered in his mind, it made him feel things he didn’t know were possible. Her touch, her warm hand gripping his. She was alive, her grim firmer than most people he’d shaken. She was new, she was exotic and he wanted to know all about her. Starting from the very beginning.

But he wasn’t going to rush things, no matter how much he desired to know. He was going to respect her wishes and stay out of her affairs until she decided that she trusted him enough to include him.

No matter how long it was going to take, he was going to wait, and he was going to have fun while at it. There was no rush, none at all.

CHAPTER FIVE

Sarah told Renee about what she'd discovered about Jacob and his stellar records across the globe. He wasn't just known, his actions were overly scrutinized and she wondered what that must have felt like, being in the spotlight always, not having the time of the day to yourself. She felt terrible but didn't do anything to explain it.

"What if I judged him wrong?" She asked Renee who looked at her, not saying a word. Renee was one of the people she loved above all else because Renee wasn't going to lie to her; even if the lie was to make her feel good.

"We all make mistakes, don't we? But then, better to make a mistake out of paranoia than make a mistake out of being naïve. You need to think of yourself first, above all else. Everybody else comes second, no matter who they are. You need to take care of yourself, no matter how selfish it seems. You're amazing, do you understand? He came off wrong, yes. Even if he didn't mean to, he made you insecure and that isn't something I can overlook, not on my life. Do you understand? I can't overlook it. I need to be 100% sure and when I am sure that he means you no harm, I'd rest easy. But for now, all these are speculations and speculations haven't helped anyone. I'm here if you need me, no matter when. I'll always come to your aid. I'm your friend and above all else, I'll protect you. Do you understand? I won't just leave you be, that's not my style. You're an amazing person and you deserve the best things in life. If you don't get them, then it's all on me. Do you understand? I want you happy, comfortable and at peace. I don't want you looking over your shoulders in anxiety or wondering when the other shoe would drop. Here, there's no other shoe. Do you understand? It's okay to feel confused here, I won't make fun of you. You're my best friend in the whole wild world and nothing on earth changes that. Not one thing."

"Thank you, Renee. You make me feel like I'm truly someone to be loved and adored. I'm grateful you're in my life, it's not every day one sees a soul sister. I just don't know sometimes. I want to be better than I am, but my paranoia holds me back, I second guess everything I do. Everything that happens to me, I make a mockery of. I get so confused, and turn to humour to lighten the load, all the while ignoring the pressing need at the deepest part of my soul. I want to be better but I don't know what better means or what it entails. I just know I don't want to remain rooted in one spot, blaming the world for my misfortune. My past doesn't define my present and my future is a blank slate. It takes a long time to come to terms with that. You've helped me see myself in the end, which is something I've always tried to do. To see who I truly am, past the façade of being me. Past the whole obstacles, my thoughts whip out of thin air."

She paused and took a deep breath as Renee just listened.

"I don't have the answers to a lot of questions. I don't even know most of those things I said or where they came from. Speaking from the heart is more intricate than I expected. Which is funny because it's meant to come out as easy as breathing. But sometimes, it hurts a lot, confronting who you are. And what's meant to become easier gets harder the more you try. It's like running up a hill but the hill is circular so you're just running in one spot for eternity, like an eternal hamster wheel. I don't want to keep doing the same thing and expecting different results. Which is not how the world works. It works with intent infused into actions. I've hated so many men, that I didn't even bother trying to talk to any of them to see if I can learn from them or anything. I guess my hatred for romanticism evolved and became downright misandry without me realizing it. How long has it been? Too long."

"Wow. This seems so... it makes me want to immortalize your words for all time because they strike a resounding chord within me. You're right, misandry isn't talked about, because men are taken as giants, able to go through anything with a stoic expression. But they suffer and I feel like I've aided and abetted the suffering process without realizing it. By judging all because of what happened to one, I've become the same thing I tried to hide from, the same thing that kept me up at night in anger, living with resentment bottles deep inside, full to bursting. I hated them, and I showed it to every man I came across. I made them know they were unwanted and even though I knew exactly how the feeling of being unwanted worked. I became my own enemy. It took a really long time to get to this point though and maybe I'm at a loss for words. I can't explain it. Thank you, Renee. Knowing I can count on you is one of life's greatest gifts to me."

Renee seemed to tear up a little and Sarah looked away, knowing that moment was private for her best friend. Renee had been... calm and very supportive, no matter what Sarah was going through. Even though they were staying together, she didn't nag or make a big deal out of things. She didn't even act like she cared if she was hurt. Which was surprising because Sarah knew that took a different kind of strength, a strength she didn't have. But thankfully, she had Renee to help light her way. And Renee did that without grumbling. She was blessed indeed to have a friend like Renee and she hoped others had their own Renee for when the voices in their heads become feral, trying to consume their essence from within.

"Come, let's get something to eat." Renee said all of a sudden and Sarah was confused because they were about to cook and whatnot.

"Okay? But..." Renee didn't let her finish.

"I know, I know what you want to say. But I want to take you out on a friendship date. Let's let our hair down. You in?" And Sarah wondered what sort of rhetorical question that was. Of course, she was in. Who wouldn't be?

"Your face tells me everything I need to know. That's good then, get dressed, we leave in an hour." Renee smiled, showing teeth. She was gorgeous, and it wasn't in a muted way. Whereas Sarah had a feral kind of beauty, an untamed sort, Renee had a soothing kind of beauty, her pale skin accentuating the beauty of her raven black hair, in comparison to Sarah's redhead. And Renee was taller, by a few inches. She was slim, but shapely in the right places. And she had a boyfriend, Brad. They'd been together for years and Sarah wasn't sure when it began if she was being honest. All she knew was that Renee had been in a relationship longer than most. She had hands-on experience about several things that would do nothing but turn Sarah's head upside down. The cool and calm way she approached situations somehow influenced Sarah too, making Sarah look at situations more objectively than she'd have done in the past.

"You're so sweet, you know that right?" Sarah said while she was at the doorway, stopping just to be sure Renee heard her.

"Aww, thank you. You're sweeter." Renee said, blowing her a kiss and she caught it. They both laughed and Sarah went to do the necessary things. Even though the date was a casual affair, they both did their best to look good because romantic relationships sometimes broke but friendships last a lifetime and a half.

"You look stunning." Sarah complimented Renee who smiled and said, "Look who's talking. You're the definition of beautiful. I'm jealous of your fiery red hair. It's like flames dancing atop your head. Goes so well with the red dress." And Sarah was forced to agree when she stared into a mirror. She was gorgeous. Fiery and maybe even feisty. She decided that she wasn't going to let that word get to her anymore, she was going to dump her bag of trauma where it belonged; out of her life.Renee was wearing a shimmering black dress with stilettos. Her hair was up in a bun, giving her a professional yet elegant look. There were teardrops diamonds on her ears and she looked regal.

"Let's knock 'em dead, shall we?" Renee said and Sarah nodded. They were both doing what was best for them, taking time off for self-care and whatever else was associated with it. And it wasn't bad, never bad. They needed that, to make sense of their existence. It was an age-old tradition, one that neither one of them had bothered to break. Once or twice a month, they went out on a fancy date, and had the time of their lives. Sure, there was nothing wrong with eating at home but their friendship was cemented on the sands of time, they were inseparable and they went to great lengths to show that to each other. It was thoughtful and just like them. Sarah was having the time of her life, if she was being honest. It wasn't just the exquisite dining, it was more of the atmosphere. The sweet but heady wine helped clear her head and loosened her tongue. She informed Renee of things she'd only thought about. can you blame me for thinking he's a stalker? Such a handsome man, and he's going after me. Not to say I'm basic or anything but he's absolutely gorgeous. And he doesn't seem to know that. Or maybe he knows it all too well. I can't figure him out. In the supermarket, he was very honest with me. He explained himself. Did I mention he speaks so well? There's this richness to his tone of voice that can't be manufactured casually. It was so him. Truly. And I loved it. Does that make me weird? Noticing his accent? It's almost imperceptible but he speaks well enough to make someone drool. Am I rambling? I feel like I'm rambling and I don't like rambling. But he's so dreamy, *ugh*."

Renee listened to her best friend speak and she was smiling inwardly. It was refreshing to see Sarah come out of the slump she'd been in for three years. She didn't know the future but she was just glad to see her best friend coming alive again. On some days, she was like a zombie; lifeless and unmoving. On other days, she was just doing what needed to be done, nothing more, nothing less. There was no pleasure to it, not one. And that worried Renee. Brad met Renee outside of the house because he knew about Sarah's situation and they didn't want to rub their relationship in her face. They just wanted to make sure that Sarah was doing well in the long run. Was it hard? Probably. But then, what were friends for? Of course, Sarah had no idea of this, she just thought Brad was extremely busy and Renee did nothing to dissuade her from that notion. Renee knew that her best friend needed a guy in her life, even if it was as a friend. And from the first day, the new guy Sarah met had been exciting, came with drama, just what Sarah needed even though she didn't know it by then. She needed to be jarred out of her slump and to embrace the unpredictability of life.

"..I don't know if I like him. He confuses me, and I don't even know him yet. He's a gentleman, yes. He's renowned, yes. But aside from that, I don't know much about him. Who he is or where he's from. Maybe I should ask him? Would that be better? I don't know, really. But he seems so friendly and when he smiles, it makes me feel a certain way, a certain way I like yet scares me at the same time. It's as though he's genuinely happy to see me, which is one thing I don't understand. I haven't been anything but trouble to him, he should be taking extra steps to avoid me and yet he doesn't, he even claims he wants to see more of me. Don't you find that weird? Odd? I don't know, it makes no sense. Maybe he's not what he seems? Secretly a narcissist with a penchant for hurting women? Okay, that might be going too far. What do you think, Renee?"

It was clear that Sarah wasn't able to hold her liquor but it had never been a problem to Renee, not once. She was there to protect Sarah, which was why they came in her car instead of both of theirs. She knew that she'd end up driving Sarah home.

"I think you'd do great; whatever it is you decide on. You think about everything and that's admirable. You don't leave things to chance, you don't even consider the notion at all. That's another thing I love about you. You are careful, very careful to avoid being hurt and that's worked for you so far. But with this new guy, you should know it's okay to try new things. He doesn't seem to want anything more from you than being friends, and I think that's healthy. You can start off as acquaintances and if that doesn't work out, you can sever ties. How does that sound?"

Sarah was almost asleep in the chair so Renee didn't get her response. She noticed Sarah on time and grabbed her because she slipped off the chair. It was a silly mistake she made, forgetting how light a drinker Sarah was. She should have rationed the drinks. She got the help of a bellboy and they jointly helped Sarah into the car. Renee thanked the bellboy and tipped him generously before driving off. A lot of people would call her rich, and they wouldn't be wrong. She'd risen the ranks of her company through sheer force of will. And she wasn't backing down. Did that mean she got people who hated her? Yes. Did she care? Hell no. She wasn't just calm because that was what was expected of her, she was calm because that was her nature. She saw life from a logical standpoint, contrary to Sarah's emotional standpoint. Which was why they were so good for each other. They were the perfect balance. And nobody tried to put anybody down. That was another thing that stood out in their friendship. There was no abasement, no condescending tone or anything. They were two different people who made living together work. Renee just wanted to see Sarah happy, that was all she cared about in the entire world. Everything else could as well take a backseat. Sarah woke up with the grandfather of all headaches, and she felt like puking. The hangover was worse than she expected, it was hard for her to open her eyes. While she moaned and groaned on the bed, she heard Renee's voice.

"Wake up, sleeping beauty." Renee said, getting a chuckle out of her. Renee always knew how to lighten the mood without even really trying, which was one thing she admired about her best friend. The ability to turn a situation around without thinking too much about it.

"How long was I out for?" Sarah asked groggily, slurring her words without meaning to. It was just that the headache was taking precedence over rational thinking.

"Twelve hours I believe. Here, I brought aspirins. And food too, in case you're feeling hungry. It's toast and tea. Would help with the nausea." Renee explained and Sarah could feel emotions welling up inside her. She didn't remember much about the previous day, but she could remember feeling safe. That was all that mattered to her.

"Keep this up and I might steal you from Brad." Sarah said cheekily as she opened her eyes to see a blurry Renee smile at her.

"Oh? I thought you already did." Renee quipped and Sarah tried to laugh but it turned into a cough instead. After calming down, she took a sip of the hot tea placed by her bedside and felt it warming her insides. It was beyond therapeutic.

"This is so good." Sarah said, pointing at the cup of tea and Renee grinned. Sarah still felt weak but she needed to eat something before taking the aspirin since it wouldn't do well to take pills on an empty stomach. The adverse reactions might cause a bigger problem than the hangover, and she knew that from being hungover one too many times. Mostly with Renee, she didn't trust anybody else that much. She was practically out like a light whenever she drank more than intended.

Although the wine of the previous day must have been stronger than she'd expected because she didn't remember drinking that much for her to be knocked out completely. Renee could handle her drinking, more than most people. Which made her the perfect person to go out with. Also, she was a no-nonsense person, and she had proficiency in various martial arts. Mostly aikido, taekwondo and boxing. She mentioned that it was best to keep the basics simple. And a few guys have had their arms wrung whenever they tried to touch Renee without her express permission. And even when Sarah was with Renee, Renee acted like a big sister, and the look she levelled on anyone daredevil enough to come within five feet of Sarah was legendary. So, Sarah knew that even if she couldn't defend herself, Renee was going to defend her without batting an eyelid. It was how they both went through university.

"Why do you learn so many martial arts? Do you expect to be ambushed?" Sarah asked one day and Renee had a contemplative look in her eyes, staring at the massive book in front of her but not seeing any of the words.

"I learned martial arts so I would be able to protect others. Like I wasn't able to before." Renee didn't clarify after that and Sarah didn't prod her to. There was this atmosphere in the room, as though Renee was begging her silently to stop the issue. So, she did.Begrudgingly though.

"You are like a teddy bear sometimes," Renee said, jostling Sarah out of her reverie. Sarah looked positively confused.

"Teddy bear? Me?" She asked, just to be sure Renee knew who she was talking to, because Sarah couldn't be sure on most days.

"Yes, you. A teddy bear." Renee said, making a silly expression on her face.

"I'll have you know I'm fierce and dangerous." Sarah said, sighing with contentment as she took a long gulp of the hot and scalding cup of tea. Her insides were warm and she seemed to have gotten her marbles.

"Yes, you are. Also, unexplainable cute. You can't deny that." Renee said and Sarah didn't feel like she was in the mood to argue whether she was cute or not, that was left to Renee. She was going to focus on finishing her tea.

"Thank you, Renee. What would I have done without you?" Sarah said as she sighed in contentment.

"Nothing, my little teddy bear. Nothing at all." Renee said and walked away to do some things around the house. The weirdest part was that Sarah agreed with that notion. She was nothing without Renee, and that was pure fact.

CHAPTER SIX

Jacob was very happy with himself. He was finally cordial with Sarah and whenever she passed by him, she didn't level him with a death stare or act like he didn't exist which was a win in his opinion. Was Diane still trying to get his attention? Yes. Did he care? No. And he was dead sure he wasn't going to. He didn't dissuade or persuade her, he let her do what she thought was best without saying a word. A lot of people would have been angry, but that was just showing an unprofessional reaction. Because Diane was good at her job, and she was an asset to the company. He wasn't going to let his personal feelings come between the growth of the company. And it was okay to like a person, there was no law stating that it was wrong. Only when it hindered productivity was it a problem. Diane's productivity was at an all-time high and strangely, he felt happy because of that. Even if it wasn't because of him. As long as she kept putting in the work, he knew that they'd have no problem, not even one.

"Hello sir, heading somewhere?" Diane asked as soon as he came out of his office, eyes trained on the elevator.

"Oh, good day Diane. Have you done the collation I asked you to?" He asked, letting her know subtly that he was all about work and nothing else.

"Yes sir, I have. Finished up an hour or two ago." She replied and he had no choice but to be impressed. She was scarily good at her job and people like her in his employ would boost productivity to an alarming degree. As long as she didn't try to mix business with pleasure he wasn't interested in.

"That's stellar. You're amazing at what you do, Diane. I'll be heading out for the day. Lock up as soon as you're done." He said with a tone of finality and she gave a small bow. He left. Sarah had been unable to come to work due to an illness and she called ahead. He was worried about her so he asked if he could come see how she was faring. There was silence for a few seconds before she agreed. He'd gotten a smaller car, so as not to draw attention. It was a BMW, unlike his Ferrari. And it made more sense to use that in a small town.

He drove to her place and wondered just what he could say. No words were coming to his head. Were they friends? He wasn't sure. But they could be friends, he knew that much. They could be, if that's what she wanted. But he wasn't going to push a friendship or a relationship of any sort, no. He knew that she got the wrong first impression from him and he tried not to make it worse. Which was why he was rethinking going to her place. He didn't want her to feel like she had given a stalker her home address but that was silly because he was responsible for company records and he knew where their houses were. It was standard protocol. Or at least that's what he told himself. He didn't think about the alternative.

He drove at a comfortable speed, noting the small houses that were all around him. Having lived in some of the biggest cities in the world, there was this allure that the small town had to him. Their company was practically the only large-scale business within a 50-mile radius. Everybody seemed to know everybody else and he found it quaint and convenient, especially since he was already fed up with the city life. There were always people up and about, moving like pendulums, back and forth, with no exact destination in sight. Nobody tried to slow down, they were all trying to rush to nowhere. He found it… distasteful on most days. He was never truly part of them, staying completely isolated from the herd mentality they carried with them wherever they went. He didn't fault them for it though, he knew that they couldn't really help the way they were, that's the indoctrination, the way they were raised.

A small town was more his style, and it let him slow down considerably. In a large city, it was hard to slow down when everybody around you was moving at a ridiculous pace. Without meaning to, you'd find yourself influenced by their way of living. A truly terrifying thought. He wondered what Sarah thought about her town, wondered what she thought about him. Even though he didn't voice it, it was clear that he cared what she thought about him and the world around her. He'd been to so many countries, and continents. One thing stood out for him; the fact that humans so far removed from civilization seemed to have a better handle on life than those who were ingrained in it. It was a truly curious thing.

He took note of many things, like the number of houses he sped past. Like the trees on either side of the highway, covering a bulk of land. He found it soothing, noting that the forests remained untouched. Even though the town had developed to a degree. The weird part was that he wasn't sure that there were up to 30,000 people in that entire town. Which was a funny thing because he was used to people being... everywhere. The big city life could be a pain in the ass sometimes. So, he felt out of his depths when he realized that the place he'd chosen to settle down was a place that he never would have imagined returning to, ever again. Life was tricky like that He pulled up at the front of the house which was Sarah's address and placed a call. He wanted to be 100% sure that he was wanted there. If not, he was going to leave immediately. Not out of malice or ego, but out of respect. Although most people couldn't differentiate between them. Sarah answered the call on the second ring and bid him to come inside. It was a homey place, with flowers planted just right outside. A bungalow, that's where she stayed. He rang the doorbell and the door opened. He remembered that he didn't ask if she could walk to the door and he felt stupid all of a sudden. When the door opened though, it wasn't Sarah. A different girl stood there, giving him a blank stare.

"Hello, good day. Is this Sarah's house?" He asked and the girl made way for him to enter. He felt strangely self-conscious, for reasons he couldn't pinpoint. The girl wasn't doing anything, not really. But he still felt as though he was being scrutinized heavily.

"Is she inside?" He asked the girl and she nodded, pointing in the direction he was meant to head. He said a thank you and with his most professional attitude, he approached the open door at the end of the hallway. The girl followed after him.Sarah was on the bed, watching a movie on her phone. She rested her back on the bed's frame, a pillow propped on her lap, a blanket covering her body.

"Hello, sir." She said as soon as she saw him and he didn't know what he was to respond to that. The blank-eyed girl seemed to be hovering around and when she made as though to leave, Sarah held out a hand to stop her.

"Renee, meet my boss, Jacob Hardings. Boss, meet my best friend, Renee. My only friend really." She explained and he could finally understand why Renee seemed so distrustful of him. She must have heard things about him firsthand from Sarah and she must have concocted her idea of the kind of person he was. Which would have been nothing short of an assumption of his true character.

"Hello, Renee. It's a pleasure." He said smoothly, knowing that there was nothing on earth that could remove him from that situation. It was clear that Renee hated him on sight even if they hadn't exchanged a word.

"Hi to you too." She said and he noticed she didn't return the compliment. Well, it wasn't that much of a problem if he was being honest. Sarah had a life different from what he expected and it wasn't his place to tell her how to feel or how to talk about him.

"Now that the pleasantries are over with, thanks for coming over. I was feeling under the weather, so I had to call in sick." Sarah explained and he nodded in understanding.

"Is your best friend sick too?" He asked and Sarah looked at Renee and then back at him and she laughed out loud. "What's so funny?" He asked, hoping he didn't miss some sort of joke. Or maybe it was an inside joke but he noticed that Renee wasn't smiling, she was scowling at him. "Oh, nothing. Renee took a day off to take care of me. Since her workplace is in a neighbouring town. I'm always grateful for Renee because, without her, I really don't know what I'd have been by now." There was sincerity shining through her words and Jacob couldn't remember having such strong feelings for anyone. One girl even called him a percher, someone who didn't stay, not really. She called him shallow too, but that could have been her prejudice shining through, in which case it wasn't his fault at all. But thinking back, he'd been aloof from the world around him, making surface even friends and connections. Nothing that really stayed, not even his past relationships. Or maybe flings would be the right term, because he was never invested in any of them. "Don't oversell it, I just wanted to relax too." Renee said with a scowl he knew didn't reach her heart and Sarah seemed to know that because she didn't even bat an eyelid, just continued cheerily. "So, do you have friends, sir?" She asked him and he wondered what the answer to that truly was. Sure, he had friends, everybody did. But was it right to call them friends? Or mere acquaintances? He had his college buddies but most of them didn't stay in touch. Or maybe he was the one who didn't, he couldn't be sure. He hadn't made time out for anyone, no matter who they were. He didn't see the point and he said as much, but only to himself. So, how was he to explain it? He chose the easy way out. "Yes, sometimes. But business calls and everybody is usually busy." By everybody, he meant himself but that wasn't a detail he wanted to share.

"So, how did you meet Renee, if you don't mind me asking?" He said, placing himself on a chair that Renee brought in. She went over to where Sarah was lying and tucked her in, almost reflexively.

"I met Renee in university. She was one of those quiet girls whom everybody respected but avoided. I didn't know why and since I had no luck mingling, I had to try my hardest to become Renee's friend. It was... a dilemma. We were two completely different people with different values. But we bridged the gap whenever we competed academically. She was really good, made me put more effort than I'd ever had into academics. And because of her, I aced all my papers, from beginning to end. We met in the library and had a silent friendship. After a couple of months, we became academic friends. Shared notes and key points. Even though we weren't always offering the same courses. I grew because of her. And I'd always be grateful."

He listened to her as she spoke, taking note of the way Renee didn't interrupt, or try to add her two cents. It was as though

Renee understood that the moment was Sarah's and she let her have it, no questions asked.

"Renee, how did we meet? How did we become friends?" Sarah asked her and Jacob heaved a sigh of relief. He wasn't sure how he'd go about asking a total stranger something so personal.

"Oh. As you said, I was a loner." She said, wiggling one of her eyebrows.

"I didn't say that, don't put words into my mouth." Sarah said with mock indignation, making Renee laugh. Jacob wasn't sure he'd seen a sweeter definition of friendship in his life.

"Okay okay. I'll be serious." Renee said and suddenly, Jacob could feel the atmosphere change. It was a curious thing, the sombre feeling that suddenly blanketed him.

“I liked being alone, mostly. I tolerated people but I had no use for them. Especially as friends. I just did whatever I wanted and left the rest. But Sarah was... persistent. She tried to get to me and after a while, I let her. She became my only friend and I became hers.” Renee finished and Jacob couldn’t deny that their words complimented each other beautifully. It was like poetry in its most sacred form. The true definition of art. And they had it. He liked listening to them, hoping to learn one or two things because of how refreshing their friendship was.

He never had that, not remotely. Maybe he indeed was a shallow pond, looking like an ocean from afar. But once people came close, they realized he was just... a guy who didn't really know what to do with his existence.

"I think..." he said, phrasing his words in a way that'd come off as inoffensive, because he genuinely wanted to be friends with her. He wasn't sure why, if he was being honest. "Thank you for telling me. It feels personal, so I'm grateful that both of you told me. I envy the friendship you both share. It's nothing short of therapeutic." He said and they both turned to look at him as one, and he could have sworn they were mirroring each other without even realizing it. It was eerie. Yet wholesome.

"I wasn't sure what to make of you at first, but you're alright." Renee said and his mind reasonably calmed down. Her hackles were no longer risen, and she seemed to have gotten used to his presence. The blank stare was gone, and he could understand why she treated him the way she did. A lot of men would have been intimidated or offended. But he wasn't one of those men.

"And you're alright too, thanks for welcoming me to your home." He said and all of a sudden, Renee facepalmed herself. He wasn't sure what he did wrong, and he was suddenly wary.

"What's wrong?" Sarah asked.

"We've been bad hosts." She said and Sarah's eyes widened considerably and he saw shame wear her like a blanket. Which was something he didn't remotely understand.

"I'm so sorry, sir. Would you like anything to eat? Drink? It totally skipped my mind." Sarah said and he smiled, realizing that they were fretting over nothing. He wasn't really hungry or anything but he realized he was thirsty, probably from the drive.

"Oh, that's nothing. I'll have water, thanks." He said, without missing a beat. He knew that they were just trying to be good hosts but he didn't think that it was something to be worried over. They needed to relax, he was fine the way he was.

"That's okay," Renee said and went to get a bottle of water for him. Sarah still couldn't move from the bed and he didn't want to think that anything was wrong with her.

“Are you fine?” He asked as soon as Renee left, forehead creased with worry. He didn’t know what was wrong with her but it seemed pretty serious.

“Oh, yes. This is just a result of a hangover. I probably took more than intended. So, it is just a result of that. But, I'm fine now. I don’t think I can handle my alcohol as well as I think. I should be back tomorrow.” She said and he wondered if she’d gone mad, even momentarily.

“Oh, no you don’t. You’re not coming back to work tomorrow.” He said, his voice having a tone of formality.

“What does that mean?” She asked, looking at him suspiciously. He realized that he wasn't explaining himself as well as well as he ought to.

"Oh sorry, I mean you can't come back to work tomorrow because you need to recuperate. I've had hangovers before and they're nothing short of horrible. So, I need you in top form when you return. You think you can do that?" He asked and she nodded, which made him calmer because he wasn't sure what he'd have done if she was being stubborn about it.

"Why are you being nice to me?" She asked him and he felt... a pang in his chest. He didn't even know why, since he was literally her boss, and he still made time off his busy schedule to come see her instead of delegating others to do it for him.

"I don't know." He answered truthfully. Because he knew that she'd spot a lie coming from miles away. It wasn't really about being friends; they technically weren't friends. They were just cordial with each other.

"That's okay, it would have been weirder if you did." She said and he cocked his head to the side, wondering what was going on in her head. He didn't know too much about her but he also knew that he didn't need to. She was at home with herself and that's all that mattered. Renee came in after that, presenting him with a bottle of water and a glass cup to go with. After he took a healthy drink, he felt like he'd gotten himself again.

"Thanks for the hospitality, I should get going. Be well, Sarah. Thanks for your time, Renee." He gave a small bow and was out of the house because he didn't want to overstay his welcome. That was what most people didn't understand, it was easy to forget that humans sometimes tired out easily. Even he forgot sometimes. So, he always put it at the forefront of his mind to ensure he didn't make a mistake that he wouldn't be able to take back; ever.

Sarah was going to be fine and that was all that mattered.

CHAPTER SEVEN

It had been a week and four days since the hangover episode and even though Sarah felt self-conscious about it, Jacob never really mentioned it again, not even to her. She didn't know what his game was but she was grateful he didn't try to make fun of one of the things she was insecure about. He'd been a perfect gentleman and didn't try to force conversation where it wasn't necessary. She decided to talk to him, broach the subject.

"Hello sir, I was wondering if you'd like to be friends." She said to him out of the blue as he walked her to her car. He always took special care to make sure he didn't touch her in any way, or make her feel uncomfortable, he took great care, in fact. He loved that fact about him. He always kept a reasonable distance between them and their conversations, even when stilted were respectable and never veered off the main point.

"Oh, friends?" He asked, as though that was the first time he'd heard the word. She wondered if maybe she was coming on too strong and tried to explain herself the only way she knew how.

"Oh, I'm not being presumptuous, it won't be like me and Renee. I just mean; maybe we'd get to know each other?" The words sounded stupid in her head and she wondered what possessed her to make such a statement. Maybe it was the mere fact that he was too kind and she was getting the wrong signal? She hoped that wasn't the case because she wasn't sure she could stand the embarrassment.

"Sure, I'll be your friend. If you'll be mine. I've been meaning to ask you, but the time didn't seem right. I'm really glad you brought it up." He said and her self-consciousness evaporated like the wind. As long as they were on the same page, that was all that mattered to her.

"Oh, thanks. I've been really mean to you, haven't I?" She said, the self-consciousness returning as she visibly cringed at her past actions. He wasn't a threat, not really.

"Nah, I don't see it that way. You were protecting your space and who could blame you? You had the right idea of it." He said, smiling down at her. Renee was tall and he still towered over her. He was maybe 6'3 and Renee was around 5'9. But Sarah was 5'2, which meant that she was a dwarf in comparison to both of them. And Jacob was smooth, too smooth. The way he talked, the way he acted, the things he said. It made her way to scream sometimes. He was perfect and she didn't like perfect, not always. But he made it seem... comfortable.

"Thank you, again. I appreciate you not holding that against me." She said and the way he cocked his head to the side melted her heart. He was beautiful, and sometimes totally clueless about it.

"Would you like to grab a coffee sometime next week?" He asked, and she was stunned. It was clearly a date and she didn't know what to think about it. But, she was done hiding from him, he didn't deserve that. He deserved only the truth.

"Let's see how next week goes, yes? I'll let you know." She said and he didn't push her for a response. Just nodded and when she drove off, he walked back to the office. She couldn't place it. He wasn't just a big shot, he was THE big shot. Known across literally everywhere. Women were practically dying for him to say a word to them.

So, why her? She didn't think she had anything different from them, not really. She was plain Jane on most days. But he, he always dominated wherever he entered. He didn't need to raise his voice, his presence was a testament to who he was. The casual grace and charisma he exuded without thinking about it. It was a lot, if she was being honest. And he didn't even realize it.

She knew that Renee would have an answer, even if she didn't. Renee was like Sarah's encyclopedia of all things. She helped Sarah make sense of the world and all its different aspects. It was a relationship that more or less benefited Sarah more and Renee didn't seem to mind. So, Sarah drove home with one thought in mind; tell Renee.

"What did he say? Oh, he asked you on a date? How bold. A coffee date? That's a good one. What was your response? You told him you'd see how it goes? Hmmm. Slightly better than a rain check." Renee was ticking the boxes in the writing pad she held, a look of seriousness on her face.

She pouted her lips as she looked over what she'd written, her forehead creased, since she was in her thinking form. Sarah liked her thinking form sometimes because it was where she could bounce most notions off Renee without coming off as offensive.

"What should I do?" Sarah asked, at a loss on what to do because if she was being honest, Jacob was a cool guy and he didn't have any sort of baggage with him. She didn't want a relationship, that was a given. But as for friendship, she realized she wanted to be friends with him. Which was a surprise because she hated the thoughts of men only a few weeks before. But now, it was as though her past hate was unfounded. It was beyond curious, even for her.

"What do *you* want to do?" Renee asked, laying emphasis on the sentence. Renee gave advice, yes. But only after a decision had been reached. She doesn't try to alter, doesn't try to make her way the only way. Sarah didn't know what she did to deserve such an amazing friend.

"I want to be his friend, and it's a shock to me." She said and Renee didn't even bat an eyelid. She wondered if Renee had somehow predicted things going that way.

"Is that really what you want?" Renee asked and she nodded in the affirmative. There was a certain shock factor to it, which was surprising for her because she didn't ever imagine she'd be in such a situation, especially with someone like Jacob.

"It's weird, I know. But strangely, this is what I want. I'm not being cajoled or anything. If he'd tried, I'd have canceled him immediately. But he didn't try, not really. He didn't push me for a response, which is something I find very admirable. Does this make sense or am I just rambling?" Sarah asked, merely to be sure because she knew that Renee wasn't going to lie to her, ever.

"As long as it's what you want, then I see no problem with it. I support it even. And you aren't rambling, you're very coherent, which is more than I can say for most people. As long as you make it clear that it's only on a friendship basis, then I think you two would do just fine. That's my take though. It doesn't have to be facts." Renee said and Sarah just rolled her eyes. Renee was rarely wrong. That's another thing that sets her apart from most people. She didn't make bogus claims to fit a narrative, not really.

"Thank you so much, I'm happy you're here. And don't be modest, we both know you're never wrong." Sarah said and Renee showed the ghost of a smile before she said, "Not always."

Sarah didn't need to think too much to understand what Renee meant, it was a forbidden name, one she tried to do her best to forget. The one who hurt her the most.

"So, how do you think the coffee date would go?" Renee asked her and Sarah had to admit to herself that she had no idea, not even one. She realized that predicting the actions of Jacob was nothing short of an extreme sport. It was better to just let things be and see the way they were going to play out.

"Honestly, I can't tell you I have a definite thought. But I believe he just wants to talk about me, probably get to know me and vice versa since I've not exactly given him leeway to know anything about me. This should be like trying to make sense of an otherwise complicated concept. I think it would be fun, somehow. I'm not a soothsayer or anything, but I can say for a fact that it would be amazing. Because of the sort of person he is. If it was someone else, then maybe I'd say something different. But as I told him, let's see how it goes." Sarah said, taking a sip of water as she watched Renee scribble some things down.

"That's the best response. I want you to know I've got your back, no matter what." Renee reassured Sarah and Sarah took it in good grace. All that was left was for the date to arrive.Somehow, she couldn't wait.It was meant to be a casual date so she wondered if she was just making a big deal out of it by getting a new dress, having her hair and nails done, etc. But Renee told her in no uncertain terms that every date was just an excuse to dress up and look good, and there was no need to be self-conscious about it.

"Are you sure? This seems like overkill." She said to Renee, taking stock of all she bought. A knee-length gown, as black as the night, with a low-cut bodice, but not too low as to seem inappropriate. She always kept track of situations like that, to avoid giving mixed signals. She liked to be straightforward.

Overkill or not, you look good. Why overthink the one thing you decided to do? Just do it, and try not to worry. I'll keep track of your every move, not to worry." It sounded like Renee said that as a joke but Sarah couldn't be sure. Renee joked, yes. But she didn't joke with safety, at all. She made sure Sarah was accounted for at all times. It was sweet, very.

"Okay okay, I'll dress up and look pretty. Let's hope he doesn't think it's overkill." Sarah replied, still overthinking everything.

"If he does, then he's an idiot. I do not suffer idiots to come within ten yards of you. So, don't worry. This is just a way to unwind. If he thinks it's overkill, then sorry for him. Let's get you prepared."

Renee meant it about the preparation, and Sarah followed along with it, as excited about it as though it was prom night. It seemed magical for some reason, ethereal too.They did whatever they wanted, playing like children in the house. After an hour of that, Renee ordered Sarah to go bathe so they'd start getting ready because it was going to take a while.True to her words, it did. It took the better part of two hours.

Jacob wasn't sure what to expect when he rang the doorbell, and he wondered if a tuxedo was appropriate attire for a coffee date. Although he didn't want their first date to be in a coffee shop, maybe after they'd been friends for a while, they could do just that. But he wanted the first date to be unforgettable. When the door opened and he met Renee, he greeted her kindly and handed her a gift box he got while on the way. It was just casual stuff for the home, but she seemed to appreciate it.

"She'll be out soon. You can wait in the sitting room." Renee said after thanking him for his kind gesture. He did as she bid, wondering what was taking time. Although he knew that women generally took more time, that wasn't a myth. He decided to occupy himself by checking his phone's mail for any pending notification he must have overlooked. While he was doing that, he heard the soft *clink* of a stiletto heel. He raised his head and his world came undone.

What he was staring at, was the epitome of perfection, humanity's crux of evolution. She moved into the light and his breath caught in his throat. She was wearing a gown that seemed tailor-made for her, and whenever she moved, it was as though the gown had become water, flowing along with her every move. She wore hoop earrings and her body seemed to come alive. He couldn't stop staring. Everything else was erased from his memory, nothing else seemed to matter. Just her, only her. And who could blame him? For the first time in a long time, he was completely dumbstruck. Or maybe flabbergasted was the word. He couldn't for the life of him figure out how someone like her was existing in the same plane of existence as he was, it made no sense.

"You're beautiful." He managed to say after a lengthy silence. His eyes took in her form and he knew deep down that he'd fallen head over heels in love with her, no questions asked. He only hoped that however long it was going to take, he'd be able to make her feel the same eventually. "And you look dashing." She said, smiling. His heart hammered in his chest and he felt like a schoolboy in front of his crush. He, who was majorly unaffected by women, had been totally bamboozled by one. One who was too pretty for words without even trying. He wanted to say something but he didn't trust his words to come out right, not really. She was... glorious.

"What are you two waiting for?" They both turned in unison to see Renee standing at the doorway, arms folded across her chest.

"Sarah, would you go out on a casual date with me?" He said, holding out a hand for her to take.

"Yes, I would. I don't know about casual though, we both prepared for something different." She said, a mischievous twinkle in her eyes.

"I think we can still pull it off. Shall we?" He said and she took his hand, running her arm around his as they left the house with a cheery wave and Renee shut the door behind them.

"You think she's glad to see us gone?" Jacob asked Sarah who shrugged.

"One never knows with Renee." And Jacob decided that from the little he knew about Renee, that was apt.

"After you," he said, holding open the car door as Sarah stepped in. After making sure she had her seatbelt on, he returned to his side of the car and gunned the ignition.

Deep down, he knew they were going to have the time of their lives. Maybe.

CHAPTER EIGHT

Sarah had no idea where Jacob was taking her, only that it was out of the town. Although she wasn't really bothered, a small town didn't always have high-end restaurants, so it wasn't that big a deal. And the reason why the town was so important to her was because of people like Mrs. Dodds. Even when their lives weren't going so great, they often had something good to say about the debilitating system of the entire world. She didn't share their sentiments, but she appreciated their outlook on life nonetheless. It made things a little less dreary, at least in her opinion.

"So, how does it feel to be so popular?" She asked him after the silence of the car became deafening. She decided to speak while they were on their way.

"I don't know, I try not to think about it." He replied, and she could tell that somehow, it wasn't a good thing like most people thought. It was more of a thing that hung over him like a bad dream he couldn't get rid of, no matter how he tried. He spoke of it like a curse from a time far removed from this one and she wondered just what he must have been through to have such a view.

"Can you explain?" She asked. She knew she wasn't meant to be firing him with questions but she was mostly just intrigued and she didn't see any harm in it.

"Sure. It's not a big deal. Sure, it seems like it is but it really isn't. People have expectations of you without informing you and when you don't meet it, they blame you for it. Something you had no inkling of an idea about. It's hard to keep friends when your every move is scrutinized." He explained as he drove and she tried to make sense of it. Being popular was one thing but being respected? That was another. And he was both.

"We're here." He said and she turned to look at the towering building before her. It was meant to be a casual date, but suddenly, she was in a five-star restaurant and everybody was acting like it was completely okay.

"I don't know if you're comfortable with this, sorry I didn't inform you sooner. I didn't want to ruin it. Honestly, I wasn't sure how you were going to take it and even now, I don't know. If you want us to turn back, I won't mind." He said and she found it sweet that he cared enough about her opinion to risk throwing a wrench in his plans that'd been on for a while.

"That's fine, really. I understand why you acted the way you did. And I didn't it sweet. I'm not mad, at all. Let's go in?" She held out a hand and the smile that broke out on his face made every single thing feel as though it was worth all the hassle in the end. She was smiling, in tandem with his smile. They struck a startling pose without realizing it. And suddenly, there were flashes going off. Camera flashes.

Oh no. He guided her through a path amongst the throngs of reporters that suddenly materialized as though out of thin air. And he led her into the building. She felt… she wasn't sure what she felt. One moment they were sharing a moment and the next, so many flashes. She was shaken but not for herself.

"I'm so sorry. I didn't know—" he tried to explain but she held up a hand to cut him short, taking a deep breath.

"How do you handle them when you're out?" She asked, startling him. He was surprised and showed that all over his face.

"You're not angry?" He asked her and she nodded. He looked at her again, still looking confused.

"I'm not angry, not even a little bit. I'm just wondering how you navigate all of this. Doesn't it get to you? How do you remain so unaffected? Can you tell me? I'm curious suddenly." She said and he smiled, a bright and sunny smile.

"That's easy. But first, let's get a table." He wasn't done talking before a waiter appeared to take them to a table on the rooftop.

"It's pretty high up." She said and he nodded in the affirmative. They weren't in any real danger, the entire thing was as safe as safe could be and he said that much to her.

"I originally didn't intend for the rooftop view but the reporters outside, some of them might try to get into the building. The rooftop is a restricted space, only for people who are in the know. The owner is a friend of mine." He clarified and she wondered if she heard right. She knew the owner of the restaurant was a big-time businessman, and he had chains of businesses across the country. The continent even.

"How do you handle the noise? Or the people?" She asked him as soon as they'd settled down on a table. He was silent for a while before he responded.

"I meant it when I said I don't handle it. When I met you for the first time, you had no idea who I was. Most people in the town don't. It felt refreshing to be seen as a human and not a quick cash-grab scheme or a way to become famous. People didn't really care who I was and the only people who didn't understand what was going on were you and a lot of people in the town. I felt... feee. As long as the reporters didn't stalk me though, they were fond of that sometimes. My home address is not listed anywhere, even in the office. I mostly take a roundabout approach when returning home. I first drop my car a long way off and then use a taxi through a different path to go home. It can be... intense. Sometimes, I want to get away from it all, but it proves impossible because no matter how I try, I'll always be a Hardings. I'll always be seen as one of the business moguls and there's nothing I or anyone else can do about it. It's just the way it is." He stared at nothing, and she didn't try to fill the silence with empty words, no. That wasn't her style. She assimilated what he was saying and it felt like she was the one who needed to apologize for taking all of what he was saying before for granted. Most people coveted fame without knowing the truth about it all. Which was funny because if they did, they'd have changed their minds.

"Permit me for asking this but… how do you survive? I've tried to wrap my head around it and it's not working as well as I'd hoped. How do you survive?" She asked again and he just laughed as though she'd said something funny.

"I don't." That was his response and she felt her blood run cold. He was suffering, and people couldn't even see it, because, on the surface, he was rich and famous. They were all hopelessly shortsighted. And they didn't even know it.

"At one point, it was fun for me. Until I realized that my life was no longer mine. Whenever I did little things in public places, it always made it to the news without fail. So, I had to take care not to bring too much attention to myself, however way possible because if I did, I'd be jeopardizing myself. My life became a spectacle, and it wasn't the good kind. It was the kind I tried to avoid by all means, although I find myself unable to. It's comical, at best." He explained and she didn't have words to help him, or to make him feel better. His hurt was... transcendental. And she didn't know how to help him deal with all that.

"I think... I understand slightly. When I first met you, I didn't really know where you came from, and I didn't really have a mental view of you. Until I saw you again. Even then, I had my reservations. I guess I didn't know you, not really. Sorry about that." She said and he had a contemplative expression on his face, as though he was looking but not really seeing anything. She didn't blame him, his life was the ideal life most people wanted, but they didn't know the consequences.

"It's fine, I wasn't ever bothered by it. Not actively. You were who you were and I was who I was. There's no point dwelling on what was, let's talk about what will be." He said and the smile he sent her way was full of something poignant, something true. She just couldn't place it, the power of such a smile. It was heady and full of a brand of mischief that most people wouldn't have recognized, especially because they weren't looking hard enough.

“We could leave here, yes?” She asked him as soon as the food arrived and he raised a single eyebrow, gesturing for her to continue.

“We could, yes.” He said, still staring at her.

“I mean without you being accosted. Your car is right outside and a lot of people would be waiting for you to finish dining and return. How would you handle that?” She asked, worried. If she was being honest with herself, her worrying probably wasn’t unfounded. A lot of things were going on, more than she could place. It made her feel... overwhelmed momentarily.

"Oh, that. I'd just have the restaurant take care of it for me. They'd send it to a different location later on. As for how we're going to leave here... I'll tell you once we're done eating. Is that alright?" He asked and she nodded. She wanted to see what other cards he had up his sleeves.

"Yes, that's fine. You're pretty resourceful, you know that right?" She said to him, expecting a smile. But he didn't smile, even the ghost of a smile wasn't present. He looked... tortured for some reason.

"I have no other choice." He said and the weight of his words hung heavy in the air, too heavy that she almost lost her footing.

It was clear that his life looked like a fairytale outwardly, but was a total nightmare inwardly. And he was handling it just fine, like a pro. Or maybe he didn't need to handle it, not actively anyway. He could just avoid the entire thing, as he'd always done.

"The food was stellar, thank you." She said and he looked up at her finally showing a smile.

"That's good, I was worried you wouldn't like it. Although in retrospect, I brought you here. It just skipped my mind that most journalists hung around places like this. Which is an oversight on my part. If this was business, it could cost at least one entire year of setbacks. I'll try to be more considerate in the future. Now that you're done with the food, I don't need to tell you how we're going to leave here, when I can just show you." He said and she wondered what it was that he had in store. She couldn't guess because she was sure all her guesses would miss the point, or not even get there at all.

"I'm anticipating." She said and he called over a waiter to clear their table. Then he whispered something in the waiter's ear and he left on a different errand, probably to find a nondescript car for them to go out of the restaurant in. But she didn't think that was Jacob's style. He didn't realize it yet, but he had a flair for the dramatic. Or maybe that was just his life. Without realizing it, he does things that would definitely put him in the spotlight.

The waiter returned and told them to come with him in the most polite way possible. They did. And on the other side of the rooftop, there was a deafening noise. She squinted her eyes and saw what seemed to be a helicopter, hovering in midair.

“Is this your idea of a simple getaway?” She asked him, trying not to laugh. He must have mistakenly the glint in her eyes for approval because he admitted that it was the only way they could get out of range of the paparazzi who were less prepared than they were.

"You're a man of many talents, Jacob Hardings." She said as the helicopter came to a stop and he let her go on before him. She knew he didn't mean to, but deep down, she was sure that they'd made one of the biggest blunders known to man. And she was going to pay the price for it eventually.

CHAPTER NINE

As expected, their little adventure made the morning papers. She wasn't angry, that would have been unnecessary. And there were two shots of them with the headline, *BUSINESS TYCOON'S POTENTIAL LOVE INTEREST OR A CASUAL FLING?*

There was a picture of Jacob covering her face with his body, and another picture of them in a helicopter, but no faces were shown. If only they'd taken a different car, none of what happened would have happened. But she knew that was how she dealt with things, not how Jacob dealt with it. But the entire thing was giving her a migraine. She was grateful it was a Friday night because then that Saturday, she didn't have work to go to. And Renee was going to be available.

"Does he realize what this means?" Renee asked and Sarah was dead sure he didn't. He probably had no idea the wheels he'd set turning. She wished she could hit him over the head with something, but maybe that was going too far. She liked a quiet life and he'd taken that away from her. Although it wasn't technically his fault, but she'd have loved a coffee date in the town instead. And maybe grab a few things from a local eatery. That would have made things so simple.

"No, I don't think so. I'm not sure he understands because if he did, he'd have known the kind of person I was. Maybe I didn't make it clear." Sarah said, bitterness in her voice. Sure, her face didn't show, thankfully. But those in the town would recognize her and it wouldn't take long for a picture or two of her in that dress to *leak* miraculously, another one of technology's wonders. She felt stupid, for believing that things could go right, if she just wanted them to. It was a childish wish, one that she didn't think through, not really. Because if she'd done that, she'd have understood so many things.

"I'm so sorry, Sarah. If I knew this was his plan, I wouldn't have let you go." Renee said, seeming more pissed off than Sarah was. She knew how Sarah acted in the spotlight, and knew that it wasn't good for her. She'd been in the papers once before, and it was a total disaster. It wouldn't take long for someone to piece the dots together and find her out, wherever she is. Which was what irked her to no end.

"I didn't know either, so sucks for the both of us." Sarah replied, more downtrodden than she'd been in a really long time. The funny thing was that she was genuinely getting to like Jacob and maybe in a year or two, she'd have considered dating him but that entire notion was thrown out of the window. He wasn't just a celebrity, he was one that the world recognized. Only the mere fact that the town wasn't on the map like other places made him able to walk freely. And it was also a town where people running away from their pay demons came to settle down. Divorced, heartbroken, frustrated, traumatized, etc. They all had something that defined them. After the whole spectacle that happened with Sarah, Renee suggested they drop off the face of the earth, and go somewhere most people wouldn't think to look. And it worked really well, for three years. Until Jacob appeared. And ruined everything.

"How are you going to get him to stop trying to see you? Because we both know there's no second chance; not after this." Renee hit the nail on the head, addressing the giant elephant in the room before Sarah had a chance to. Which was another thing Sarah was grateful for. Renee was all facts, no matter how it seemed. She didn't sugarcoat things to make anyone feel better. Instead of doing that, she just kept silent. Which was another way of preserving peace.

"I will talk to him. We can be friends, but no more dates. And maybe reduced time together. He's thoughtful and sweet, yes. But he's not doing his best when it counts. Granted, he doesn't know about my past. But still, the helicopter business was a no-no. It became blown out of proportion because of it. Going on a second date would mean something worse probably, maybe ten private jets writing letters in the sky. I don't need that kind of notoriety. Not now, not ever." Sarah could also be honest with herself, especially when it was time to rip the bandage off. She didn't try to deceive herself, she found it distasteful, and utterly unnecessary.

"I thought you'd say that. I didn't want to be the one to suggest it. But first, let's see how the news is taken by some of his many admirers. If they try to cause trouble for you, let me know. They'd be down faster than they can call 911. I don't like seeing you in this state, so maybe we'd do something about that. Forget about him for now, let's go somewhere, just the two of us. With disguises, of course." Renee said and Sarah began to consider the idea. Not only was it feasible, but it was smart too. And it was going to help her get the taste of the day before out of her mouth.

"Let's do this." Sarah said and Renee slowed down before saying, "It's a two-hour drive. You sure?" She was always so thoughtful.

"Yes. The farther the better. Sarah replied resolutely and when Renee saw that she'd made up her mind, she smiled.

It was time to go on an adventure.

~~

Thinking back, Jacob realized that something was wrong when he saw the morning papers. He tried to place a call to Sarah but it went to voicemail instead. He went over to her place but neither she nor Renee were around. He was worried because things were... totally different from how he originally planned. It was meant to be a quiet dinner, but there was nothing quiet about it, it made the front page of a few newspapers, and even when he tried to shake it off like it was nothing, he had a feeling that he'd created something, unlocked a Pandora's box and threw away the key.

But there was nobody for him to talk to about it. Which is why he called Diane on a whim. She picked on the first ring.

“Hello, Diane.” He said, hoping his frustration wasn’t showing through the phone. For all he knew, his life was technically a nightmare. And there was nothing he could do about it.

“Hello, sir. This is the first time you’ve called me since you’ve gotten my number. Does it have anything to do with the newspaper article?” She asked and he realized that she must have recognized Sarah. Most of the townspeople must have.

"Oh, right. That's one, but I just wanted to talk to someone." He said and almost beat his head because of how stupid he sounded. She wasn't a rebound whenever he made a colossal mistake, he didn't need to treat it as that.

"I'm here, sir. You can talk to me." She said and he sighed in relief. Although it wasn't outwardly. He didn't want to come off as creepy from over the phone.

"Assume it was you on the papers. How would you feel?" He asked and for almost fifteen seconds, there was no response. He was wondering if something was wrong with the phone.

"I have different values. And, I might enjoy the notoriety for a while, but no longer than one or two weeks. I love being in the spotlight only when I can erase myself from it, if need be." She explained and he realized that he'd been selling her short. Not only by assuming she was a gold digger when she was maybe just attracted to him, but by assuming that she had nothing going for her.

"That's pretty detailed. Can you tell me how you'd act?" He asked and the silence was even longer this time, but he was in no rush. He could practically hear the gears turning in her head from over the phone. So, he just waited until she was ready.

"If it's not with my express permission, I'd hate it. If I'd known, then I'd have been better prepared and maybe even wave to the camera. But it didn't seem that way, not while you hid Sarah's face." Diane said and he felt his blood run cold. She knew who it was without him saying a single thing about it.

"How did you know it was her?" He asked, even though he wasn't sure he wanted to know the answer. He needed to do damage control but what was he to do? Apologize? To who? The world? Sarah? He couldn't make sense of it anymore.

"It was clear. You've been hanging with her for a while, so who else would you go out with? I just want you to know that Sarah isn't me. You don't really know most things about her." Diane said and he could feel himself getting livid.

"What do you mean by that?" He asked, trying to control his frustrations at the happenings he unwillingly orchestrated.

"You'll find out for yourself. If that'll be all sir, I should get going. I have a ton of things to work on." He clearly knew when he was being dismissed and it stunned way more than he thought it'd have.

"Oh, right. Sorry for calling out of the blue. Have a lovely day." He said and ended the call without even waiting for a response from her. It was clear even to him that he'd botched a lot of things news. He let everything go to voicemail. He didn't care that much, not really.by going out of his way to be romantic when Sarah didn't expect such from him. The weirdest part was that she didn't care how rich he was, and yet... he flaunted it without even meaning to.

He could see his faults, and they were astronomical. His business line had been ringing all day, with most of his clients asking for details and whatnot. Some advertising agencies wanted to run adverts on him while he was still hot on the

He wanted to undo what he did but how could he? Sarah wasn't available and Diane seemed peeved. He didn't even want to think about how Renee must look by then. She was probably going to tear him apart the next time she found him.

He could have called his contacts and asked for the story to be taken down but he knew how futile that was. It was also stupid because as soon as he did that, he'd create another narrative, one he wanted to steer clear of. He wished his brother was around, his older brother who wanted nothing to do with his father's wealth, a free spirit. He hadn't heard from him in over six years and sometimes he wondered if he'd made a mistake, letting his brother go that fateful day. It was a heated discussion and he said some things he shouldn't have, some things he was paying for.

If you can hear me, brother, please find your way back home.

But he knew that was just a prayer to the wind, a wish without a hold. And it was just him trying to make sense of the mess he'd created, nothing more and nothing less.

People said that mistakes were made a lot less when you got older, but that seemed to be the reverse for Jacob. He made more mistakes the older he got and people weren't like numbers, they were too complicated. With numbers, 2+2 was always 4, no matter the time or season. But people, their 2+2 changed with how they felt. They could be 4 today and 0 tomorrow. There were just a lot of changes that sometimes, he couldn't keep up with them, even when he tried his hardest. He'd watched people, he'd seen them do things that made no sense from a logical standpoint. And they somehow tried to justify their actions. It confused him, made him wonder if maybe he was the one created *wrong.*

They didn't often have a set path before them but before he could walk, he was already able to have conversations with numbers. He kept it under lock and key for a few years but even while trying to hide, his talent or whatever it was, shone through. He was called a prodigy and it didn't matter how complicated an equation got, he could see the number dance upon a page, feel their emotions, and understand what they were thinking. He could reach out to them and they could do the same for him. He often tried to think about how that much has seemed to others but realized that they didn't see it the way he did and that no amount of explaining would really do anything. So, he stopped trying to. People were always around him, doing things. They always did things he found difficult to understand. And everybody else around him seemed to be in on it. It was as though there was an inside joke and he was the only one who wasn't privy to it.

A lot of people tried to befriend him, even date him. But he couldn't understand them. And mostly, just frustrated them with his efforts. Some left, calling him shallow. One stood out like a sore thumb.

"When will you realize you can't keep using this excuse, while hurting people around you? Even a month-old child should know better. You're not a child, you can't keep using the fact that you don't understand the emotions of others to hit them where it hurts the most. That is devilish in ways I don't want to think about. Fix your act,

Jake. And then, maybe you can come find me. Until then..." and she walked away.

It'd been two years since then and he hadn't seen her again, or tried to enter into another relationship. Sarah was... different for him and he'd botched it without even meaning to. It was a poetic sense of justice in a way, a sense of justice that made him laugh and wonder if the world was conspiring against him. He didn't know how he felt about Sarah. He liked her, yes. Maybe loved her? Or was that just being in the moment? But trying to understand her was proving harder than ever. He decided to try again though, a muted affair, not pushing or prodding or trying to outdo himself. He just needed her to return.

That was all he was asking for. Nothing more, nothing less. She was a friend, a good friend of his and he didn't want to ruin that with his own brand of issues.

But how could he explain himself? Listening to Diane had shown him that Sarah wasn't simple, she wasn't surface level. Of course, he knew that but he had a vague idea before. Now he realized that while he was a shallow ocean, she was the Atlantic Ocean, with depths that kept going, no matter how far he tried to reach.

But he couldn't give up, he couldn't afford to. But he wanted the entire thing to blow over on its own accord, and maybe he'd be able to talk to her and get coffee as they originally intended. He didn't know what was going to happen in the future and if he was being honest, he wasn't sure he cared as long as Sarah was fine and he didn't mess up things in her life too much. If he did, then that would be nothing short of messed up, and he didn't do messed up, he never did.

He was many things, but an idiot was what he wasn't and if Sarah needed space, he was going to give it to her, no questions asked. But he was worried. Who wouldn't be in such a situation?

Maybe you really are bad for people, Jacob.

He tried not to believe that, but he just couldn't shake it away. He knew deep down that something was terribly wrong but he needed to give it one more try, to prove to himself that he could be wrong too.

Numbers were alive in his hands and that talent, he was willing to pass it on to see if he could understand humans like that too, starting with Sarah. It was a pretty high place to begin, but it was better to start somewhere than to not start at all. He only hoped she was going to forgive him for all he was putting her through without meaning to.

"I'll do better, I promise." He said to the empty air and this time, he held himself to that, knowing better than to just do things on a whim. He needed to go slow and see what the world had in store.

Until then, he was content to wait. Numbers were eternal anyway.

CHAPTER TEN

One thing Sarah was grateful for, was the women in her workplace, the women in her town generally. Her pictures were never released to the press, and the women began to protect her with even more ferocity. They were intent on letting the past not repeat itself and she was beyond grateful for that because she didn't know what she'd have done if one of them had betrayed her and sent her pictures over. The men were mostly obtuse and they wouldn't have recognized her anyways. Women paid more attention to such details than most men which was good because it was hard to get the loyalty of the men, especially when you weren't giving them anything in return. Which was precisely why she steered clear of them.

"Good morning, Sarah. How're you holding up?" Diane, one of the women she could actually trust came up to her while she was in the bathroom washing her face. She smiled brightly when she saw Diane because she knew that Diane was someone who'd protect her probably more than Renee would.

"I'm fine, thanks for asking. It's really been a month since then, hasn't it?" She asked, staring at her reflection in the mirror. She couldn't believe everything had blown over so easily. The newspapers probably got bored when they didn't get any more scoop and moved on to other pressing matters.

"A month, yes. How do you feel?" Diane asked and Sarah stared at her reflection in the mirror, wondering what was true. She wasn't sure how she felt, she'd been avoiding Jacob for an entire month and they hadn't really talked about what transpired. She wanted everything to completely die down before she talked about it. That way, there'd be nothing to trigger her.

"I am not sure. I know how I felt an hour ago, but I have no idea how I feel now. Emotions are funny things." She said and Diane just smiled in understanding. Diane was beautiful, but she had a hard look about her, as though she'd wrestled her demons and come out on top. For all Sarah knew, that was probably the case.

"I get that. Tell me if you feel something, yes? And don't worry about Jacob. He's harmless. I've tried to get into his head and it's true what they say. He's all numbers, and can't comprehend the workings of people. I thought it was bogus at first, or maybe he was playing an elaborate prank on you. But he's genuinely just a confused guy. Maybe I was too hard on him." Diane said and Sarah shivered inwardly as she thought about what Diane must have put Jacob through. She wasn't known to hold back her punches, no matter the opponent.

"Don't give me that look, I'm serious. He's really naïve, and doesn't understand how the world works. He thinks big equals to good. Which was probably why he took you to such a ritzy place. He didn't understand. I'm sure he still doesn't. You can punish him for it but it wouldn't make a real difference. He's many things, but he's not a bad person. He can't even be if he's paid to act like it. His understanding of the world from what I've observed is more or less from a silly standpoint. He doesn't feel the things others do, and even if he does, he translates it to binary like a computer to better understand it." Diane spoke and the information that came pouring out of her was information that Sarah wouldn't have gotten in a thousand years.

"How do you know all this?" She asked, at a loss for words.

"You have a silly memory, but it's fine. I was a spy, once. And now, after changing identities, I think this is the life I want to live." Diane replied and Sarah remembered when the women of the town she knew came together and shared their stories. They were spies, trauma survivors, women running from serial killers and God knows what else. The town was a safe space because it looked normal on the outside but the women in it could potentially ruin any man's life with a flick of the wrist.

They had a bond, a bond of knowing. Of sharing pain, of understanding the inner workings of it. And Diane was one of the people she bonded with back then. She trusted Diane with her life and she knew that Diane trusted her too.

"So, do you suggest I keep being friends with him? Is that it?" She asked, merely to be sure she understood the situation.

"Yes. That's precisely what I'm saying." Diane replied, not sugarcoating her words. She was as straightforward as Renee sometimes or even more so. Diane wasn't afraid to hurt anybody's feelings.

"Why?" Sarah asked.

"Because he needs it. He's a fish out of water, technically living on dry land. The ways of the people are alien to him and whenever he tries to understand or make sense of it, it falls by the wayside. He needs a guiding hand, a friend. And I know you like being his friend, you can't hide that from me." Diane said and Sarah was shocked at the accuracy.

"But, what then? Just a friend?" She asked, her brows furrowed.

"Yes, just a friend. He can't handle a relationship, no matter how much he thinks he can. He'd make decisions that no woman would tolerate, no matter how rich he is. And sometimes, he'd do the dumbest things. Which is why you have to leave it on a friendship basis. Do you understand?"

Sarah didn't need any more talking to, she understood vaguely the kind of person Jacob was. In the world of nerds, he was king. In the real world… not so much. She thanked Diane for her timely words because if she was being honest with herself, she was about to throw Jacob out the window of her life and not look back. Sure, it was going to hurt but she thought it was the safest bet.

Now, all she needed was to tell Jacob and hope for the best.

~~

Jacob needed to talk to Sarah, he just wasn't sure how to go about it. She didn't return his calls and mostly avoided being in the same room with him. And since he'd promised himself not to make her uncomfortable, he had to stick with that, whatever the cost. Sure; it didn't make sense in the grand scheme of things but he knew that if he tried to push things, she'd totally disappear and he'd never see her again.

Cambridge was way easier to understand than Sarah, at least to him. They were like-minded people there, the only problem was that, they thought they were the same as him. They weren't. And after realizing that they were creating cliques or whatever for those like him, he made sure to avoid every single one of them. They couldn't understand him, not really. They could try, yes. But it was an exercise in futility. That showed with the way they banded together for a common cause. He didn't understand people, but apparently they did.

He really would have preferred friendship with Sarah, she was refreshing in ways he'd never explored before and he didn't want to ruin that, which was why he kept his distance.

And just while he was about to lose hope, she came to him.

“Lost in thought again, aren’t you?” She said and he couldn’t believe his eyes. She was standing in front of him, and didn’t look like she was positively going to murder him. He wasn’t sure if that was a good thing or not.

“I’m sorry.” He said, without thinking about it because he knew deep down that he offended her. She just smiled and said, “That’s water under the bridge. Let’s get coffee sometime. Real coffee this time.”

She said and he smiled sheepishly, knowing he'd been caught red-handed. He agreed and they shook hands.

And that began their friendship. He didn't try any extravagant gesture, keeping it simple, no matter how much he wanted to blow it out of proportion. With numbers, the bigger the profit, the bigger the business. But humans didn't work that way, at all. And he was learning.

He noticed that Sarah liked her coffee black, and wondered why. She told him it was a habit she formed many years ago. He also noticed that she favoured her left hand over her right, but she was ambidextrous. She could write with both hands as cleanly as ever. She also was a lover of sappy romance novels, it took a while before she fessed up on that one.

With every new layer of her he discovered, he realized that there was more to see, more to explore. She had layers upon layers to her, like the programming of a top-secret vault. Whenever he thought he'd hit gold, he found a solid, almost impregnable door waiting for him. It was exciting, getting to know a person from the base.

He learnt that she was a simple person, one who loved simple gestures and nothing more. She only liked extravagance when it was coming from one of the women she loved so much. She claimed they understood her and he suspected that was true.

Ten coffee dates later and they were walking hand in hand, laughing at one of the viral memes of a cat when the most impossible thing happened.

He saw his brother.

He froze, staring at the more mature version of the boy who left all those years ago. Standing beside him was a guy, maybe a few years older than Jacob.

And Sarah was staring at him like she'd seen a ghost.

"Hello, brother. It's been a while." His brother, Daniel said, and he wanted to run. He wasn't sure where he wanted to run to, but seeing his brother so abruptly after all these years was enough to scramble his perfectly working brain.

"Hello, Sarah. I'm back." And just as the other guy spoke, Sarah turned tail and just… walked away. She didn't look back even once.

"Who are you and what did you do?" Jacob was pissed off, and he ignored his brother for a second. The new guy obviously did something to Sarah and he wanted to know what it was.

"Little brother, she didn't tell you? This is her ex-fiancé, David, my best friend. You need to keep up with the times." Jacob felt his blood run cold. He didn't know about an ex-fiancé, he didn't know about anything and that hurt more than he could have explained, even to himself. Especially to himself.

I never really knew her, not once.

And he realized that all the time he thought he was finding layers to her, it was all an illusion. He wasn't even aware of who she really was.

“Don’t antagonize David. I saw your stunt in the papers and David recognized his ex-fiancée he’d been searching for. For about two years now. We can’t talk about all of this here, where do you stay?” His brother asked, taking charge of the situation as always. He was always the first choice to handle their father’s businesses, but he didn’t care a whit about any of that.

“Let’s go.” Jacob said, resigned to fate. If his brother had returned, then there was about to be a total overhaul of the life he knew. There were just some things that you could never really prepare for.

~~

Sarah ran as soon as she was out of sight, her body shaking uncontrollably. Seeing him again, it was like a fire was lit at the core of her soul, and nothing else remained.

Seeing the man that walked into her world and turned it completely upside down. She didn't know what to think, everything was flying over her head in record time. She was at a loss for words and so she found herself in the nearest safe place and called Renee to come get her.

Before the memories did.

She stood in front of the church, wearing a wedding gown, her smile wide enough for all to see. She was beside herself with happiness. All these while, she'd pinched herself over and over again, hoping she wasn't dreaming. She really wasn't. There was a certain sense of humour to that, knowing that she was going to be wedded to the most beautiful and most amazing man in the world. He was her entire universe, and thinking about him always made her feel giddy. Her chief bridesmaid was Renee, and having her there accentuated the fact that it was the best day of her life.

But then, she began to hear murmurs, murmurs that weren't discernible at first but after a while, she was able to get snippets of the conversation. And they weren't pretty. They mentioned that the officiating minister of the wedding couldn't go ahead with it because the bridegroom wasn't present.

She was confused because she knew really well that he was never late, not David. She was worried something happened to him, something terrible. And suddenly, the day that began with so much joy started to turn into something straight out of a fever dream. Her hopes were dashed and she couldn't muster up the words to ask what was wrong.

Until someone screamed "he left a note" and that cemented it for her. She didn't bother to read the note, knowing fully well that it was going to be an excuse or another for missing his wedding.

The happiest day of her life had suddenly morphed into one of the days she wanted to forget, one of the days that she wanted to put behind her.

When Renee hugged her, she cried and this time, there was no end to it because those weren't happy tears.

Not by a long shot.

"I'm here, I'm here." She heard the voice of Renee holding her and saying those words over and over again, and she opened her eyes, red from tears to see Renee staring at her, her whole body poised for a fight.

"Where is he?" She asked and Sarah wasn't sure what to say. She didn't know where he went or why he had a godforsaken smile on his face when they met. But the feelings at the pit of her stomach were more real than anything else she'd ever experienced. And that was another source of torture for her.

"I don't know." She replied, drained beyond anything else. She wondered how Jacob was holding up, seeing his brother once again. It was not news that his brother left the world of the Hardings and went to do his own thing. She wondered how seeing him again after so many years must have felt like to Jacob. But she couldn't worry about Jacob, she needed to worry about herself first. She was going through things that were messing up her head. She just needed to rest.

"We can find him later. For now, let's go home." Renee said and led Sarah into her car, but the backseat this time, so she could lie down. Sarah was grateful for having Renee, she wasn't sure she'd be able to do life anymore if she didn't have Renee to keep holding her head above the water.

Seeing him again was nothing short of an electric shock of several hundreds of thousands of volts. Jacob was beautiful, yes. But, David was a god compared to him. And also the most handsome man she'd ever seen. His green eyes, they housed a piece of the universe, a giant chunk. And those eyes staring at her again... they shattered every single wall she'd built over the years, they made nonsense of her forced misandry.

Those eyes shattered her defences as though they were as flimsy as paper. She couldn't even bring herself to hate him.

He's so beautiful.

She found herself thinking, over and over again. How could she forget such a flawless being? He'd grown even more since the last time she saw him, a manlier version. And every thought flew out the window the moment she saw him. His effect on her was nothing short of devastating.

She couldn't tell Renee about how she was feeling because it seemed unfair to her best friend who'd done practically everything to make sure that Sarah was away from all the buzz that came with David's antics. She couldn't tell her best friend that she'd never stopped loving him because it didn't make sense, even to her. It felt like a cop-out, like something teenagers did. And she was no teenager.

But seeing David again made her feel like one. He was larger than life and he consumed her every thought. From the ground up. She wondered if that's what being in love meant, pining for someone, even if they were the source of your PTSD. She couldn't understand why forgetting him was so hard, she'd forgotten most of the things that happened to her, left friends.

Now, she had a sisterhood, not just friends. They were family. She wondered how they were going to react to David appearing out of nowhere. The world was tiny indeed, she couldn't have imagined that David's and Jacob's older brother were best friends.

They were going to shake the entire town, with or without meaning to and somehow, she knew that running away wasn't going to do anything, not really. She had to face it, and see where it was going to lead.

No more running.

~~

Jacob didn't know if he was seeing right. His brother, the one he used to look up to, the one person he could say understood him, had returned from whatever hell he was holed up in and he was acting like all was right in the world. He was in Jacob's house, a two-storey mansion. He was pouring himself a drink from one of the wine cabinets, specifically the ones that held wines of 20 years and above.

"What exactly are you doing here? And why now?" Jacob asked, trying to figure out his brother's motives. Daniel had always been a leader, even when he acted like a nonchalant child. He always knew how to get through to people in ways they hadn't discovered themselves. And even Jacob was susceptible to his charms.

"Use that big brain of yours, little brother. It was given for moments like this, yes?" Daniel said and poured a glass of wine for David. They both seemed so chummy, that Jacob wasn't sure what to make of their friendship. It wasn't really a disturbance, he just found it very unnerving how they came at that particular time and acted like nothing was amiss.

"Don't do that. You can't just waltz back into my life and think all is right with the world. I'll have you know I proved you wrong. I was able to understand people and make a name for myself. No thanks to you." Jacob said, seething with rage. But Daniel acted oblivious to it, as though he didn't just say something.

"Little brother, you should know better by now. You didn't prove me wrong, not once. You acted exactly as I predicted for you to act. You made a name for yourself, yes. But you've always been brainy. Can you look into my eyes and tell me for a fact that you understand people?" And that, was the problem. Jacob hoped that his brother wouldn't have noticed but apparently, his wishes were more or less lost to the wind. Again.

"What does it matter? Does it have anything to do with why you're here?" He asked, trying to turn the tables on his brother, as he'd seen or read about in most fictional works. But his brother didn't flinch.

"Drop the mock act of indignation, it doesn't suit you." He took a sip from the glass of wine he held and made a comforting sound. "That hits the spot. Now, where was I? Oh yes, you asked if it matters. Yes, it does. I've been following your progress, or should I say lack of it? For a while now. You haven't learnt anything. Humans aren't numbers, and they never will be. You can't compute their actions just from a few interactions. You never were able to. And I don't fault you for that, I just felt like you'd have done better, given the years. But you haven't learned anything, not as much as you should have by now. I suppose it's my fault, partially. I left to help you grow and grow, you didn't."

Jacob was tempted to punch his big brother, but that was probably what he wanted. He wanted to get a rise out of Jacob and if he succeeded, then Jacob was only going to play into his hands and be treated like a puppet on the strings of the master puppeteer.

"I can see you're getting angry, don't be. You're all logic, aren't you? Don't act contrary to your nature on account of me. That'd make me feel bad, you know. Do you know why David is here?" Daniel asked, pointing at his best friend who raised the glass he held in acknowledgment.

"No. And I don't want to." Jacob answered but Daniel waved it away like a pesky fly. Nothing could get to him, as it was before.

"David is here to do what you couldn't. You fumbled. Only staring at the picture in the newspaper, one could see from her posture that she was scared. But you, being ever so logical probably didn't spot it. Correct me if I'm wrong but the helicopter was your big getaway plan, wasn't it? And how did that work out for you in the long run?" Daniel was hitting him where it hurt and Jacob wanted to pummel the living daylight out of his big brother. It just didn't seem fair that the one person who was supposed to have his back was the one person tearing him down.

"Why are you doing this?" Jacob asked through gritted teeth, anger forming a home in the core of his being.

"What am I doing exactly? Telling you the truth? You need a healthy dose of truth every now and then, it would keep you sharp above all else. And you shouldn't fault me, you were the one who made the mistake, not anybody else. You do not understand body language or casual emotions. Your conversation skills are abysmal at best and you're making no efforts to improve. I worry for you. Worry that you'd be old and grey with nobody to love you. Not me though, I don't care for such frivolities. But ask yourself, little brother. What do you want? I'm not asking what your brain wants, I'm asking what you want. Think about that and give me an answer." Daniel said and swiped Jacob's phone before he could react.

"Hey David, your ex-fiancée's name is Sarah, isn't it?" David concurred with that and Daniel got her number in record time.

"No emojis. Plain name. At least you didn't add a full stop this time, so maybe that's progress." Daniel said and Jacob was at a loss on how he let his space be violated so thoroughly.

"How did you get my password?" He asked, because it'd been six years and he knew that he'd changed his password at least ten times after then.

"It's easy enough. I just tried the day you became a manager at the company here. You have a thing for dates, it makes you predictable. And patterns. Even when writing a lengthy password, I can tell how your brain works. It's not hard, really. You just overthink everything and end up taking the simplest of approaches. If I were a hacker, you'd be bankrupt. Good day, little brother, let's meet again."

And just like that, Daniel and David left the way they came, leaving a confused Jacob in their wake.

CHAPTER ELEVEN

It'd been years since Daniel saw his little brother and... He was still disappointed by what he saw. There was no visible change, not really. He didn't like to bully, but sometimes it was necessary to make people sit up. When he was younger, he was called a prodigy, but he rejected the term, whereas his little brother embraced it and made it his identity without realizing it. It made him wonder what would have happened if he tried to steer him on the right path. He just watched and maybe that was his mistake. The term *prodigy* came with a heightened sense of self bordering on narcissism and only a few could break out of the hold. His little brother believed that he couldn't understand humans and Daniel couldn't imagine hearing such bullshit in his life. It was plainly propaganda most people concocted to separate themselves from others and the funny thing was, they often began to believe in the lie they created.

He knew that it was going to lead to unintended consequences in the long run, but he couldn't always show his little brother the way. He needed to watch and see what happened. Apparently, it only got worse. He knew of his brother's past relationships, knew they didn't last because he claimed to not understand emotions or people. That was the laziest excuse Daniel had ever heard and he was the master of excuses, being able to concoct them straight out of thin air to get out of a fix or a responsibility.

“Do you think I was a little harsh?” He asked his best friend, David. They’d been together ever since he went AWOL. At least for three years. And they were alike in so many ways, it was eerie.

“It’s not my place to say, but if it was, I’d say no. Most people just need a huge dose of reality every now and then. David replied. They were rich, reasonably. They both owned a company under different aliases and expanded without doing much. David wasn’t that well to do when he met Daniel, but when they clicked, it was as though a world of possibilities opened up to him. Daniel was a daredevil, he wasn't scared of taking risks, always going all in and laughing the loudest whenever he lost. He was a free spirit and because of him, David was able to throw away his inhibitions and begin to create a legacy.

"Eh, let's see if he learns. Are you going to go to her?" Daniel asked him and he could see the gears turning in David's head. They were too alike, facing things head-on, grabbing the bull by the horn and not balking even in the face of opposition.

"I'll call her and then ask to meet. I don't know what her response would be, but I'm not giving up." David said and Daniel smiled. Indeed they were alike, and that's what made the entire situation worth it. David wanted his girl back and Daniel wanted to help his little brother. It was technically using one stone to kill two or multiple birds. And they were going to have fun while doing it, he knew that much. Because that's how they were and that's what made them stand out from the others.

Daniel believed that having fun on the job was what made the job interesting. If not for that, it'd be as plain as day. He didn't like plain. Not at all. Life had so many different ways to be lived, living it one way was nothing short of uncreative.

"Okay, call me once you're done. I need to look around the town, and see what I can get. We'd see where the road eventually leads." Daniel said and shook David, going his merry way. He wasn't really worried about David, he knew that David could handle anything.

Well, almost anything.

~~

David never stopped loving her, even when he left. But he knew he couldn't show his face to her again unless he had solid proof that he was going to be able to take care of her. He didn't believe that love didn't need wealth to stand. That was silly, at least from his viewpoint. Did he mean to leave her at the altar? No. But he did anyway. And he wasn't sure he'd be able to forgive himself if he was her. It was like making a joke of her. It was a scandal that was almost impossible to forget. Which was why he had mixed feelings about the entire thing. Did he love Sarah? Yes. But was what he did fair? Hell no. In fact, he knew that if one of his friends did it, he wouldn't have been able to forgive them.

But sometimes, only the one wearing the hat knew how it felt. Only he knew that the pressure was compounding. What was meant to have been a simple wedding morphed into a massive one, one he had no control over. He couldn't do it, not really.

The memories haunted him too, and every day he prayed she found someone else, someone better. Better, because if it was someone worse, that would have defeated the whole purpose of him leaving in the first place. He took a deep breath and placed a call. The call was answered on the first ring.

"Hello?" Hearing her voice made every single thing worth it, it was as though he'd been doused with a calming breeze, and his thoughts flowed freely.

"Hello, Sarai." There was only one person who called her that, and it was him. Just him. Nobody else.

"David, is that you?" She asked from over the phone and he took a steadying breath before replying.

"Yes, it is." He said and there was silence on the other end of the phone, he could only hear her breathing.

"How did you get my number? Where?" She asked and he said, "A magician never reveals his secrets." He heard her chuckle at that.

"I called to let you know that I was truly sorry for what I did to you. You didn't deserve that, and I put you through it. That was callous of me. It's fine if you never want to talk to me again, I just... really wanted to hear your voice." He said and he heard a sharp intake of breath.

"Davi... I wanted to hear your voice too." She said and he was glad that he waited a whole day before calling. They shared secret names and they were more or less attuned to each other without even realizing it.

"I'll call you tomorrow. Is that okay?" He asked and this time, there was not even a second delay.

"Yes, that's fine. Talk to you tomorrow." She said and the call ended. He didn't know what the future had in store but he didn't care. Only one thought reigned supreme in his head;

To get Sarah back.

Everything else took a backseat.

~~

Hearing his voice... was something she couldn't explain. She didn't care how he got her number, only that he did. She didn't care about so many things she had huge worries about. David had returned and that's all that mattered. Did he hurt her? Yes. He did. And she wasn't sure what he was there for. But she also didn't care. Hearing his voice again was therapeutic.

"Hmm, you seem to be in a good mood. Thankfully. Why are you smiling so sheepishly?" Renee asked, coming from behind her. And she didn't like to lie to Renee but until she figured out the main reason that David returned, she couldn't give any coherent answer.

"I don't know, I am just happy, I guess." She said and Renee looked her over, before deciding that she was already late for work.

"You are almost done, yes?" Renee asked, her motherly instincts kicking in. Sarah nodded.

"Just need to grab my bag and I'll be out." Sarah said and Renee waved her goodbye, going ahead.

Sarah left immediately after.

When she arrived at her workplace, Jacob was there. But this time, he wasn't even looking at her. He didn't look her way once, throughout the entire morning. She wondered what it was she must have done wrong, maybe something that he wasn't saying.

She decided to ask Diane.

“Maybe his brother’s arrival messed him up? He doesn’t even want to talk about it. And oh, he’s such an eye candy.” Diane said and Sarah rolled her eyes. Diane was a hopeless flirt sometimes.

“How did you even know about that?” Sarah asked and Diane just winked saying, “I have my sources.”

Jacob had that air of detachment throughout that day and whenever she tried to approach him or anything, he found a way to evade her, and it was making her worry. He was her friend above all else, and she didn’t want him to feel like she neglected him. That was the direct opposite of her intentions. But he acted like she wasn't even there. It was a sad thing and she didn't know how to bring him out of it, so she left him alone for that day. She decided to broach the topic later on because since she'd known him, he'd been always polite and maybe a little confused but never cold. Never.

And that was the problem. He wasn't that sort of person, it was as though something happened, something that completely messed him up in ways that she couldn't decipher.

But she knew he'd come around, eventually. For now, she had to figure out a way to talk to David again.

~~

Jacob was... livid. And he wasn't sure why. Maybe it was because of his brother's self-satisfied smirk, or maybe it was the way he spoke to him, or maybe it was the mere fact that Sarah wasn't... his. He knew that much, but seeing the reality dropped onto his lap was enough to shatter his perception of reality. A lot of things were not making sense and try as he did, he wasn't able to make any of it make sense.

The David guy, he knew about him. He'd researched and he found out just why Daniel sounded the way he did. The David was the one who jilted Sarah and made her life hell. He'd read up on it, and it was… ultimately disgusting. He couldn't believe someone would do such to her, to someone as sweet and as amazing as her. He was… a lot of things. And he couldn't compute all of it.

It was then he realized he didn't know anything at all about her, not actively. She didn't tell him anything, she didn't. And that hurt more than anything else. He couldn't explain how badly it hurt, there were no words for it. Nothing really could assuage the growing pit of despair in his stomach. And he wasn't sure that he wanted anything to.

That was the funny thing about it.

And he knew that with the way she acted, the David guy still meant something to her and he wasn't sure how to resolve the two conflicting parts of his brain. On one hand, he wanted to do whatever it was going to take to win her, but then he wasn't sure if that was what he wanted or what the presence of David brought about in him. David wasn't someone he liked, he wasn't going to fake it for the sake of it. And he had had it with his brother calling him little. He did what was necessary, he made a name for himself above all. And he didn't baulk in the face of clear opposition. He moved with intent and that was one thing that he knew he had going for him. He didn't second guess his actions, not really. Whenever he moved, he made sure it was the only move he wanted to take, or at least the most favourable move at that moment. He had contingency plans, yes. But those plans were seldom used because of how good he was at reading the numbers. The path, the steps, whatever they were.

Yet Daniel came from nowhere and made nonsense of all his efforts, as though he hadn't been through a lot to get to where he was. His big brother needed a reality check and Jacob swore to himself that he was going to give it. He wasn't the little boy of before anymore, he was a fully-fledged man, capable of making his own decisions. And he didn't need anybody's input in his life, not when he was doing so well.

The emotions Daniel evoked in him were threatening to tear him asunder. Which was one of the reasons he often didn't like being near his brother. Daniel could piss off a priest in ten seconds if he wanted and he'd escape with little to no consequences. He just knew how to get into people's heads and make them do his bidding. He did it without a care in the world and even though Jacob didn't approve of his brother's methods, he couldn't deny the fact that it was effective.

He couldn't remember why in God's name he wanted to see his brother again because, in the space of a few short minutes, his brother had successfully ruled him up more than anybody else ever had in years. Only he had that ability, to turn people against each other at the drop of a hat. His words, they were said so flippantly that, it's hard for you to forget even if you wanted to. He doesn't let you, even for a single second. That's what made it hurt even more.

He knew nothing about Sarah, yes. But his brother had no right to make him feel like an utter fool. So many things had changed and he wasn't a fan of being treated like he was a schoolboy with a knack for getting into trouble; as though he was some sort of recalcitrant child. He hated it immensely. And Daniel knew that for a fact; which was why he used it as a weapon.

Daniel didn't have a specific purpose for whatever he chose to do, at least in Jacob's opinion. He just found a way to cause the most havoc and leave whoever it was trying to piece the pieces. He didn't care about collateral damages, not really.

Jacob wasn't so irresponsible, at least he didn't think he was. But then, he decided to examine all his passwords and his blood ran cold. They were all the same. Or at least in a recognizable pattern. Dates. Daniel was right, he was too predictable.

That didn't make Jacob any less peeved though, it served to worsen it. Which was why he acted out of his nature, or his character. He ignored Sarah's attempts to speak to him, even while his heart hurt as he did so. He couldn't afford to let his brother be right, not while he still had so much to do. He needed to prove himself above every single doubt that he was a person who could take care of himself, with or without his nosy brother. He didn't need someone looking over his shoulders and correcting his mistakes, he didn't even want to feel like he was making mistakes.

"What's this? Stewing in the darkness like some sort of supervillain? Doesn't suit you." That damned voice. He recognized it. It was Daniel. And even after he changed the passcodes, Daniel still waltzed in as though he owned the place.

"How..." he didn't even know where to begin asking the questions, so he just trailed off.

"How did I get inside? Let's see. It's simple enough if you try not to overthink it. I made you angry and you decided to make some changes. You decided to prove that you were unpredictable and I was wrong about you. So, you just used letters instead. This time, it was Sarah Reeds. Which is, purely unoriginal if I might add. Do not go making someone yours just because your ego was bruised. It doesn't seem very logical now, does it? Also, you tried to make a statement with it, to show that you're not going to give up on David. And you'd still actively go after Sarah. While I find that commendable, have you thought about what you actually want for yourself? Not what's projected for you or what's expected of you. Think about what *you* want. I don't really care about you hating me, as long as you find your *why*. If you hate me because it was projected on you, then you're even stupider than I gave you credit for. Also, I came to take a bottle of wine, having a girl over tonight. Don't forget to lock all the doors and windows, little brother. I'll see you later."

And again, Daniel left without Jacob getting a word in edgewise. Irritated was a mild way of explaining what he was feeling. Because he felt rage from all sides, across all angles. He didn't know what to make of it, it was the first time he'd been that angry; the first time he genuinely wanted to bash his brother's face in.

But, is that really who you are?

He hated the voice in his head on most days, especially days when he just wanted to act on his impulse but it forbade him to. Like him trying to give his brother a piece of his mind, but being struck dumb. Life was funny like that. And utterly annoying. He didn't know who to blame, or even if there was someone to blame.

So, he didn't do anything. There was really nothing to do.

CHAPTER TWELVE

Planning to see David again was the highlight of her day, if she was being honest. Sure, he did a lot of questionable things and made her feel like trash for the longest time, which was why she wanted to see him and find out the truth from him. None of that lovey-dovey bullshit, she needed it straight. She wasn't stupid, no matter how much her heart yearned for him. She needed to be sure of his intentions towards her, especially with the way she returned.

And when she got to the park, he was waiting, seated on a bench. He wasn't doing anything, just staring at his hands.

He hadn't seen her by then, so she took the time to admire how finely he was crafted. His powerfully built body, his fingers that she remembered framed her face once and spoke of a love that lasted forever.

She didn't make a move to destroy the illusion in front of her, she wanted to stare at him just a little while longer, without him noticing. And then, he raised his head and his eyes met hers. All thoughts immediately drained from her head, she couldn't think, couldn't see right. Her mouth went instantly dry and her heart was racing erratically in her chest, as though trying to jump out.

"Good to see you, Sarai." Hearing his voice in person packed more of a punch that she had to sit down before she swooned. The effects he had on her were nothing if not intense. They totally shook her to her core. She couldn't think, and forgot to breathe. But all of this was happening within her, she made sure to keep her face expressionless, to make him know she meant business. It was one of the hardest things she'd ever had to do.

"And you too, David. You called me here." She said, going to the meat of the matter immediately. She wasn't a fan of beating about the bush, it usually reeked of unseriousness.

"Yes, I did. I wanted to talk to you. About what really transpired. But I didn't know if you wanted to hear it, so I called you here, just to be sure." He said and for the first time since they met again, she could hear a hint of uncertainty in his voice.

Should I make him sweat a little? Nah. Better to do this and get it over with.

"I'm all ears." She said and sat down on the opposite end of the bench. He noticed it, but he didn't say anything, it was up to her to do whatever she wanted.

"I left. On our wedding day. I didn't inform you or anyone, I just upped and left. That was mean, yes. But there's a reason. I didn't know if I could take care of you. Sure, you didn't really care about money, but I did, more than I'd like to say. And the wedding guests kept compounding. It made me confused. Because you were mostly spending your money or your family's to foot the bills. I wanted to call a halt to it, mainly because I preferred a small affair with your family and mine but I could see the way you shone, the way you excluded happiness. I was just out of a job by then, so you did most things alone, without complaints. I felt useless. Like the one thing I was meant to do, I couldn't even do it because it wasn't feasible for me at that time. I wanted to rant and rave, but to who? I wasn't even listening to myself. I decided that I wasn't good enough for you.

If I failed so heavily at the beginning, what was the hope of even becoming better? I know everybody thought it was just a phase, but I became more depressed than I'd ever been. And everything seemed to be going well for everyone, except me. I didn't want to steal your smile, not when you worked so hard to put it there and you accepted someone like me without a second thought. It felt unfair to you, and I wanted to be better, but then, how could I? The wedding was already underway. So, I left a note. Someone else got it apparently. I didn't mean to leave you, but if I didn't fix myself, how was I to be of any good to you?"

He went silent for a while before continuing.

"I was a coward, I couldn't face the unknown. I didn't want you to hate me, I really didn't. But I decided that the life you deserved, I wasn't able to give it to you. I just... failed. And failing at life was one of the worst crimes known to man. I failed and there was nothing exactly I could do about it, failure had become a part of me. When I saw the newspaper article, I was broken. I returned a month or two later but you were gone. Nobody knew where you were and most people who were there for the wedding either tried to spit on me or set me afire. I couldn't go to your family's house, I wasn't sure what I was going to meet there and I was also sure you weren't there, so I didn't want to poke the hornet's nest for nothing. Not only was it stupid, it was something that even an idiot could see was a bad idea. So, I left. And that's where I met Daniel. He was friendly, extremely and told me not to give up and all that. He started working on something with me and before I knew it, I'd found my mojo again. It took a long time but working with Daniel was what eventually sealed it. I enrolled in a gym, and started to take better care of myself, all the while still looking for you. He told me to not rush it but it was still a lot to process. I wanted to run after you, but he reminded me that I didn't have where to look. He was right on all counts. So, I focused on building myself and looking for you alongside. If you were married or in a serious relationship when I found you, I promised myself to leave you be. I didn't want to ruin whatever you had going for you."

She listened to him with rapt attention, not interrupting even for a single second. She let him talk, to say everything he had to, not holding back. She still didn't interrupt. She understood where he was coming from, she just didn't know how he expected her to be cool with all he'd said. He was practically the person who made her see men as terrible people and now, he was telling her something completely ludicrous, she was tempted to laugh.

“And? Why have you returned?” She asked him, unable to keep the coldness from seeping into her voice. Her eyes went cold and she stared at him, unfeeling. She wasn’t sure he deserved her forgiveness, nor after all he’d put her through.

“I just wanted to see you again. I know this is stupid of me and you’ve been kind enough to not throw me out, for which I’m exceedingly grateful. I just really wanted to talk to you, to be with you. I know I hurt you, and I’m sorry. I didn’t mean to, not that way.” He said again and she walked towards him and slapped him across his face.

"Do you have any idea what you put me through? Do you vaguely understand it? You claimed to love me, you claimed you weren't going to leave. And now look at precisely what you did. You *fucking* left a note. A note, for crying out loud, David. That wasn't just stupid, it was immature of you. And you're right, you're a coward. You can't confront your problems and look to others to solve them for you. No, I won't be your Guinea pig, not this time. I won't be the one you call one when everyone else forsakes you. You made me cry every single day, shattering myself. Hearing the name David triggered me, it became a banned word. Seeing men with your height made me turn my tail and run in the opposite direction. Where do you get off on saying you're sorry? Is that supposed to let you off the hook? You messed with my mind, royally. And I'm meant to hold out a hand and say I forgive you, and I welcome you back into my life? This is real life, David Sanderson. And in real life, you face the consequences of your actions. Don't call me. Ever. Goodbye."

And this time, Sarah didn't look back. She walked away, even as her heart shattered into a bazillion pieces and she wasn't sure she'd ever be whole again.

But it had to be done. For her sanity.

~~

Jacob met with Sarah for coffee and decided to apologize for the way he'd been treating her.

"I'm sorry I went cold on you. My brother, he messed with my head. He made me dredge up certain emotions I wanted to leave buried." Sarah noticed the bitterness in his tone and decided to coax the truth out of him.

"Do you want to talk about it?" She asked him and after mulling it over for a few seconds, he decided to speak.

"My brother is a genius, so most things are a joke to him. Either he doesn't care, or they're not enough to catch his fancy. He messes with people and somehow gets away with it because he's the golden boy and the golden boy gets away with everything. He knows how to read people and you must have noticed I don't. Don't worry, it's not really a secret. Ever since we were younger, my brother tried to get me to show more emotions than I was used to. He tried to get me to understand my feelings. Even if it meant hurting me just to make me feel. He was... a complicated teacher. He'd hurt me with words and whenever I came after him, he just evaded me like it was nothing. He claimed I was too immersed in people's idea of me to think for myself and one day six years ago, I told him to get out of my life and see if I wouldn't make something of myself. He did just that, contrary to what I thought. He declined any offer to take over the company and just disappeared. For the longest time, I felt guilty about driving him away. I wanted him to return. He was my only sibling. And now that he's returned, I'm tempted to tell him to leave again. He's still trying to get a rise out of me, and I fear it's working, which is the biggest problem here. It's not meant to work, at least not on this scale. But even after all these years, he can still affect me heavily. And I hate that."

She wondered how long it must have taken for him to come to that conclusion. She knew that it was hard and if she was being honest, she wanted to run away sometimes too. And with David's return, she wasn't sure what right or wrong was anymore. She thought her feelings from before had morphed into hatred but that wasn't true and that irked her to no end; so she understood exactly what Jacob was talking about.

"Have you tried telling him to just let you be yourself?" She asked, wondering why he couldn't just send his brother out and not feel guilty about it.

"I have. He doesn't have a listening bone in his body. He believes his way is best and doesn't try to give me a lot of reasons why I can't do stuff without him. It's beyond annoying. I'm not little anymore and I need him to stop treating me like some mannequin, one he needs to direct their every step. It is one of the things I despise the most about him. He's a perfectionist, but he doesn't need to project his perfectionism on me. Makes me wonder if we're brothers or just playing pretend. I don't like things this way, but he doesn't listen to reason. No matter how I try." She could see that his dilemma was similar to hers and that made them kindred spirits, of sorts. She wasn't really sure.

"If I were you, I'd tell him off completely. But you're not me, neither am I you. Do what works for you and if he doesn't like that, that's on him, not you." She said, hoping he'd understand that he didn't have to change for anyone, least of all for someone who tried to direct his every step. He was in charge of his own life and it was up to him to decide who was going to be in it and who was going to be out of it.

“Enough about my overbearing brother. What about you? How’re you handling your ex’s return?” Hearing it phrased that way made her cringe inwardly but she decided to tell him the truth because he did the same for her too.

“He apologized, for everything he did in the past. For leaving. I don’t know if I can forgive, I don’t know if I want to. He just came back into my life without so much as a heads up and expected me to flow along with it like he didn't make nonsense of my life before. It makes me wonder what's true and what's false. What I took to be true was him, and he ended up being false. So, his return, I don't know. I don't want to think about it. It makes me angry anytime I do. I don't want him looking for me, not actively anyway." She fiddled with her thumb, lost in thought.

"I can understand. But I want to tell you something." He said and she looked up, wondering what made him take on such a serious tone.

"Okay, go on." She said, urging him to continue. She strangely wanted to hear what he had to say.

"I don't know about your ex, and I know it's a sore topic for you, but I think I like you, Sarah. Or rather, I know. Being your friend, it's fun and some days I don't want it to end, sometimes I just want to bask in that moment for as long as possible. What I'm saying is, that being with you makes everything make sense to me, I don't have to second guess things, not while you're here. Your existence, it makes mine feel valid."

Sarah wasn't sure of how to respond to such a blatant expression of love, especially when she was trying to heal from David. She decided not to blame Jacob though, she knew that he didn't see things the way others did, so he wouldn't have known that was one of the worst times in the history of worst times to spring something like that on her. She was dealing with one emotional baggage, she wasn't sure she had time for another.

Jake was cool, and friendly too. But she was confused. She didn't know what she felt for him, couldn't understand how deep it went or how shallow. And that was the major problem. Jacob was confusing. Without meaning to be. She didn't have a response for him and even though she felt bad, she didn't want to outrightly lie.

"Can I talk to you about this some other time? Please?" She asked, wanting him to drop it. Thankfully, he did. But she could sense the awkwardness of the atmosphere, so she left after a couple of small talks that had no substance.

She couldn't commit, at least not then. And she wasn't a fan of deceiving people. Leaving Jacob in the coffee shop was her way of being merciful.

She wasn't always merciful.

CHAPTER THIRTEEN

Sarah wondered if it was possible for a brain to combust due to the information it was being fed. Or maybe for her brain to lose track of itself because it was being pumped with information from all sides. She decided to talk to the one person who was there at the origin; Renee.

She was the only one who knew Jacob and David at the same time. And there was nobody else Sarah trusted than her. At least not on that level. She trusted Renee with her life, the part of her existence that she didn't joke with, she trusted Renee with that too.

"I need to talk to you." She said to Renee as soon as she got home, to see Renee sitting on the floor, legs crossed.

"Shoot." Renee said and Sarah decided to give her the low down of what happened. She told Renee about Jacob's proposal to her and David trying to get back into her life.

"That's worse than a dilemma. It's not something that someone like you should be saddled with. But let's not cry over spilt milk, what do you want to do about this?" Renee asked and Sarah gave it some thought, realizing that there was nothing. She was stuck.

"I don't know. That's the worst part. If I did, maybe this wouldn't be so bad. But it is. It is, and I have no idea what to do. I'd like nothing more than to throw David out the window, but I still have a soft spot for him and I'm not so sure about Jacob. He's perfect the way he is; yes. But he does certain things that make me wonder. Like ruining a perfect friendship bonding moment, because he wanted to tell me he liked me. That was the wrong way to do it, and I still have mixed feelings about it. I like David a lot, I doubt I've ever loved anyone this much. Which is precisely why he annoys me so much. He hasn't been here, he hasn't seen me suffer. All because of him. I know he went through stuff too, but what he did to me, was infinitely worse. I don't know if I can see him as someone I love, or someone I want to be with. I'm totally confused."

It was hard to admit it but Sarah knew Renee would understand. She wasn't straightforward with Renee before, but Renee didn't mention it. She let people do things at the pace they were comfortable with, and didn't make a big deal out of it. That was precisely the kind of person she was.

"In your confusion, who would you say gets you the most?" Renee asked and Sarah didn't have to think about it. She voiced it out even before her brain processed it.

"David. But that's probably because we've spent the most time together." Sarah said and Renee became contemplative.

"Okay, and what are Jacob's redeeming traits?" Renee asked and Sarah had to think for a while before responding.

"He's very respectful, doesn't try to touch me or act improperly with me. He's a perfect gentleman, and soft-spoken too, he doesn't need to be loud." She said and Renee brought out her writing mad, jotting some things down. Sarah knew better than to ask.

"And does David have these same traits?" Renee asked. Sarah didn't need to think again.

"That was what endeared him to me in the first place. He was very respectful and sweet, never doing things based on ego or anything." Sarah responded, wondering where Renee was going with all her heap of questions. She couldn't really tell, if she was being honest. The questions just flowed into each other in reckless abandon.

"So, what would you say are David's flaws?" Renee was still jotting when she spoke.

"He was scared of commitment. And he left me." She replied.

"Aside from that, anything else?" Renee asked again and Sarah had to think long and hard before replying in the negative.

"Let's move on to Jacob. What are his negative traits?" She asked and Sarah didn't need to think too much because those were the things that were already irking her to no end.

"He doesn't really know how to read a room. He makes decisions based on his personality, not giving room for other people's ideas. For one, he didn't ask if I wanted a fancy dinner, he just went ahead to plan it. He doesn't take notice of most things, unless it's pointed out by a third party. He's an amazing person, but he hasn't really connected with me. We're good friends, don't get me wrong. It's just that... he doesn't make my heart flutter or give me butterflies. I get genuinely excited to meet him, yes. I don't hide it. He's fun to converse with and I love seeing how his brain works. But when it comes to a relationship, he just doesn't get the most basic of things. And that can be really frustrating." Sarah had no idea when she began to ramble, her words coming out in hurried tones. She was feeling something, she just wasn't sure what it was.

"In your own words, who do you think is a better fit for you?" Renee asked and that was just the question that Sarah had been dreading because it was like opening a can of worms. She didn't want to do it, but lying to herself wasn't going to help anyone, not really.

"David. Obviously. But... he left me." Her voice reduced an octave, as she realized that he'd never not been in love with David, even after he left. She had loved him, pined for him and her heart was beating for him. Nobody else but him.

"At least you're being honest with yourself. Do you think he has changed? Truly? Not the sycophantic kind of change." Renee asked again and Sarah had to begin analyzing her interactions with David. For one, he seemed more subdued, somehow.

"Yes. Which is one thing I didn't expect myself to say. He might act all smooth on the surface, but I can see how scared he is. He isn't sure what he's doing exactly, but it's clear he wants to make things right. He's using the wrong approach though, but I commend him for the effort. He's trying to befriend me again, the proper way. I just don't feel like giving him the time of day after all he'd done. I feel messed up because of him and sometimes, I want to scream. Seeing him again, it released something that had been caged within me for the longest time. And I just... wanted to hold him. That's what annoys me. It's as though my heart doesn't understand the facts of life." Sarah grumbled but Renee only showed the ghost of a smile, which was a big thing by her standards.

"Your heart probably doesn't care about the fact of life, and it probably ever will. You should stop thinking about the concept of right or wrong, it doesn't work in situations like this. You need to understand what your heart wants. Everything else just gives the placebo effect, and they don't remotely compare to the real thing, which is probably why you feel so frustrated. It's understandable, more than you think."

Renee usually had the answers, even if it was answers she didn't want to come to terms with because of what they'd mean in the long run. That was what scared her the most. That the answer was David.

"So, it's him." Sarah said, resigned. She knew deep down, she just wanted someone else to point it out for her. Renee didn't do that, she just made sure Sarah came to the answer by herself. Which was one of the thing Sarah loved the most about Renee. She didn't put thoughts in anyone's head, she let them create their own conclusions, no matter how bad or good it was. As long as it was truly theirs, she had no qualms about it.

"I believe in you. And remember... make him suffer." Renee said, a wicked glint in her eyes. Sarah didn't need to be told twice, she knew exactly what she was going to do even without the input of Renee. She wasn't going to let David off easy, never. He needed to pay for his actions, no matter how much she loved and adored him. He needed to pay, that was the only way she could rest easy.

~~

David knew it was over. He put on a tough exterior but she shot him down so hard, he knew that there was no coming back from that. He realized that he deserved it, everything that was happening. Leaving her on the altar was one of the most stupid things he'd ever done, and if he could have taken it back, he would have. But in real life, there were no takebacks. And he just had to come to terms with the fact that the one person he loved above all else, was no longer going to be in the picture. She was going to move on, she was going to forget him. The hurt was too much for him to bear.

He thought that he'd passed it but... she made him understand that there were feelings that couldn't be outgrown. He stayed on that park bench for a couple of hours after she left, not knowing how or where to go from there. His world had ended, and the rest of the world went on like nothing happened. They lived, they loved, they had the best of times. He couldn't have that, not anymore. He was clearly someone who was going through hell and nothing could save him by then. He wasn't sure he wanted to be saved.

He left that day as soon as it was evening and returned the next, at a loss for what to do next. And the day after that. He wasn't sure why he was doing it, he just knew that somehow, that was the one place that made sense to him.

"I knew I'd find you here." He heard a voice he thought he'd never hear again and he saw Sarah coming towards him, and he wondered what he'd done wrong. She wasn't smiling, and her chief's bridesmaid and best friend was with her. He knew from experience that Renee was one person that nobody could afford to toy with.

"Is anything wrong?" He asked, wondering if he'd somehow gotten drunk or done something unforgivable. He didn't have blanks in his memory, so he wasn't sure what exactly was going on.

"Not really. Before I accept you back into my life, you need to talk to my family and convince them yourself. I won't help you do that, it's for you to figure out. After that, you need to make sure they understand the reason why you've returned, the full reason." She said and he was reminded of an avenging angel, if the angel was a redhead. She was even more beautiful than he remembered.

"I can do that." He said, unable to believe his good fortune. He was tempted to go to her place with flowers after she shot him down but he knew deeply that it was one of the worst moves to make. No matter how he wanted to reach out to her, he needed to obey her wishes. And he was glad he did.

"Why exactly have you returned? What do you want from me?" She asked and he could understand why she was skeptical. He did create a trauma the size of the

Empire State Building for her, due to his cowardice and negligence.

“I want to go ahead with the wedding.” He said without missing a beat. She sucked in a breath and Renee looked like she was ready to kill.

“I know it’s not feasible, but I want to at least try. Not doing anything would be infinitely worse off. I want to make things right, even with the newspapers. I did a lot of damage to you, and I know that an apology isn’t going to suddenly wipe the slate clean. So, I’ll try my best to erase the shame I brought upon you.” He explained and he hoped that she could hear the sincerity in his voice because deep down, he was worried that his words weren't being passed across as he intended. He didn't want to come off as arrogant, that was Daniel's style, not his.

"That's going to take a while. Are you sure you want to do this?" Sarah asked and he replied, "Yes, I'm sure. 100%."

"And you won't bail when the plans are underway? This is going to be at least two times bigger than the original plan, if not three times. Are you willing to see it through without a word of protest?" He didn't need to worry about that part, he'd had to come to terms with that over a year before then, knowing that it was going to take over a year to right most of the wrongs he committed, at least outwardly. The inward ones were going to take a little bit longer.

"I'll see it through. You can have Daniel and Renee hold me to that. Even the police, if you wish. But I will see it through." He replied, his voice resolute and strong. He wasn't going to back down, the love of his life was within touching distance. He missed her, more than he'd ever missed anything or anyone. He missed her so much, it hurt. He didn't want to ever leave her side for that long ever again.

"Can I add something?" Renee spoke up and he wondered what sort of horror she was concocting for him. Knowing her, it was probably something that he was absolutely going to hate.

"Yes, please. You and I are as one." And that sealed the deal. If he wasn't able to do what Renee asked of him, he was going to lose Sarah. The thought chilled him to the bone.

"That's so sweet of you." Renee said, her face softening as she talked to Sarah. Then, the hardness her eyes took as soon as she looked at him was enough to make a grown man shiver.

"First, you won't touch her at all. Not even a hug. It doesn't matter how long the wedding is going to take, you're going to keep your hands to yourself, and your body to yourself. Secondly, I am always watching. If I deem you unfit to wed her, I'm calling everything off. Is that a deal?" She said and he felt his heart sink to the pit of his stomach. There was no way around her ironclad rule, she made it very specific.

"Deal!" Sarah said cheerily, sinking his heart even further. But he knew he deserved it, they had every right to mete whatever punishment they wanted out on him. He hurt the both of them, and they deserved to seek retribution.

"Thanks for helping me piece my thoughts, Renee. Let's go home." Sarah said and turned to me saying, "Let's hope for your sake that you're equal to the task presented before you. If you aren't... let's hope it doesn't come to that." And she walked away, hand in hand with Renee like a couple of school girls.

School girls with enough power to ruin his life. And they didn't even need to try.

~~

Sarah felt good, better than she'd felt in a long time, whistling as she went to work. Renee was in a good mood too and who'd blame them? They just gave themselves absolute authority over David's life and they were loving it. She especially loved how his eyes almost burst out of their sockets when Renee stated in explicit terms that she could call off the entire thing whenever she wanted, no matter how far along it was. It meant she controlled all the cards and she could act as she deemed fit without needing to worry about certain things. Sarah found it very refreshing and she said as much to Renee.

“Let’s see how he goes about bypassing rules, now when the rules are written in stone. He unwittingly placed himself in the precariousness of the situation currently presented before him. I should feel sorry, but I don’t. I feel elated even. I want him to experience most of what he made you pass through, even if it’s a little. Then; he’d have a better grasp on his words and actions. Saying the words don't mean anything if they aren't backed by hard actions. This is one test I'd thoroughly enjoy giving." Renee sounded like a sadistic person but Sarah didn't really care, she knew that everything Renee was saying or doing was for her benefit above all else. Even if it seemed callous, it was to ensure that something like what happened in the past never happened again. She was going to make sure of it and after she did that, she was going to go to great lengths to make sure that Sarah was having the best life possible. Anything else was unacceptable.

"I can't get the way he looked like a lost puppy. But yes, serves him right. He should know that his return doesn't mean much until he proves himself beyond every reasonable doubt that he's not the deadbeat he was and he's going to be an asset, not a liability in the long run. I can't keep making mistakes, and he was my greatest mistake. It's time to turn the mistake around, and chalk it all up to experience." Sarah was feeling really good about herself when she remembered Jacob. She hadn't given him a response.

"I know that look, what's on your mind?" Renee asked, spotting the change in facial expression almost immediately.

"Nothing, nothing. I'm just thinking about Jacob. He did ask me out, and I never gave him a response. I chose to avoid it instead. Was that fair to him? Or was I doing the same thing that was done to me?" She didn't know right front wrong anymore, not really. Because she realized that sometimes, the lines were so blurry that it was hard to see out of it. She just knew that she wanted Jacob as a friend and she wondered if that made her selfish. She said as much to Renee.

"No, it doesn't make you selfish. You're being realistic and that's something most people can't ever get. You need to be realistic because of all you've been through. You plan for every contingency, every mishap. And with everything you do, you make sure that you're taking the path most true to you. That's what makes it so admirable. It doesn't make you selfish or whatever, it makes you wise. And being wise is not a crime. Nor will it ever be. I'm proud of you for choosing to walk forward, despite all the mishaps and confusion. Even when you don't know the right thing to do, you do whatever comes naturally to you and you don't apologize for it. You terrorized men, and it was fun to watch. Your misandry phase made most men steer clear of you or they were downright wary of you. They were used to weak women, women with weak wills. You showed them that your mind was as sturdy as a bamboo and as flexible. They have nothing but grudging respect for you. And you did all of that by yourself. I can't help but be proud of you." Renee said, ruffling Sarah's hair. It was such a silly gesture that she didn't even realize when she did it because her mind wasn't at that moment.

"You treat me like a princess sometimes; and that makes me know how others ought to treat me, especially someone I'm going to be romantically involved with. You always make sure I don't settle for less, no matter my station. Thank you for inferring value upon me. I know you do most things out of consideration for me, and I don't take any of it for granted. You're truly amazing, Renee Karla Smith." Sarah said, hugging her best friend who was at a loss for words. So, she didn't say anything and they stayed in the hug that seemed to last forever.

CHAPTER FOURTEEN

Jacob knew deep down that Sarah wasn't going to accept him, even after he'd gone ahead to create a certain profile of her. She was untouched by his gestures, he knew. And she was trying not to avoid him in the workplace but he couldn't help but avoid her. He didn't want to hear the words he knew were coming, didn't want to hear it from her mouth before he found out from a different source. That was what was going to hurt the most, he knew it.

Even though he tried not to think about it, he knew that she was special to him, in more ways than his mind could grasp. She made him attuned to her existence and then he realized that she wasn't his. Even when he came outrightly to tell her, she didn't give him a reply at all. He'd gotten the reply he wanted after all. The one he tried to avoid, but he knew that there was no avoiding it. So; he created a story in the deepest recesses of his mind, a story where she explained that he wasn't the one for her. A story so close to the truth that it might as well be the truth.

He liked Sarah, he wasn't sure why but he knew he liked her a whole lot. And he also knew she didn't like him, at least not the way he liked her. He liked her smile and the way she laughed. He liked the way she drank her coffee and the way she carried herself with poise and grace. He didn't want to say he liked everything about her because he knew that wasn't the entire truth.

He didn't like her choice.

"Why so sullen? Do you miss someone?" He didn't need to bother asking who it was, he knew it was his brother. After changing the code two more times, he gave up and just left it like that, since it was clear his brother was practically in his head.

"As a matter of fact, I do. But, you'd say you expected it, didn't you? You expected me to miss her. Since you're always inside of my head, you know my every thought. Why don't you just live my life and let go of yours?" Jacob knew he sounded unreadable but he didn't care, he was way past caring about what his brother thought.

"I didn't expect that. You're being honest with your emotions, that's a first. Does it hurt? Make you want to hit something?" Jacob gritted his teeth as his brother spoke, knowing that he wasn't going to be able to hold back on hitting him, no matter how much he tried.

So, he stood up and swung a fist. It carried the weight of his existence on it, the weight of his frustration at always being a second choice: even to his father. Daniel was first choice, he'd always been. What use was being a prodigy if you're always going to be a third wheel in your own life? An afterthought, a spare.

That's all he was.

When he threw his fist, he expected it to connect to something but it met empty air.

"Channel your anger, don't act like a flame consuming everything in its path. Harness your rage, and find out what it's trying to teach you. Do not swing unless you know you're going to hit a dead ringer. Unless you're 100% sure, don't throw a fist. Anger can be expressed in many ways, but I believe that you understand anger without direction or understanding doesn't solve anything. I've lived on the streets, I've faced the barrel of a gun, the shade edges or daggers and different types of knives. I understand that rage at the wrong time can get you killed. Use your rage as a weapon, exactly how you harness your brain power. If you let it run amok, it's of no use to you; just a silly brain with knowledge that'd do more harm than good."

Jacob wondered if his brother realized he was technically in trouble. He was teaching

Jacob, yes but what he was teaching him was nothing short of the moves that Jacob planned to use against him.

"Your body is a weapon, and your mind can bring it under your control. You're the puppeteer of your own life. Why do you let silly things try to drag you under? Do you understand what I'm telling you? You're not random, your brain power is one of the reasons why you should stand above, but you seemingly don't want to. I know what you can be, the question is... do you?"

And it suddenly clicked. Everything that Daniel was doing, was teaching him. He wasn't just putting him down for no reason, he was trying to make Jacob see that life had different things to it, and it was not always straightforward as expected. Sometimes, it was never straightforward at all. And it took a long while for Jacob to finally understand.

"Is this what you mean when you tell me that I never grew? Because I use my brain one single way, and nothing else?" He asked, taking a fighting stance.

"Now, you're getting it. It's not enough to have big brains, you need to use it to do whatever you desire. If you say you cannot understand humans except in binary, then why don't you tell your brain to convert their words and actions? Their mannerisms? There's so much you can do, if you stop letting who people say you are get in the way of who you were born to be. I can't do half of the things you do, I'm sure most people can't. And you do them effortlessly, without breaking a sweat. Do you understand how amazing that is? That's why I push you more than others, why I say things to rile you. I don't mean to hurt you, Jacob. I'm sorry if I always do."

"You called me by my name." Jacob said, surprised. Daniel just gave a rueful smile.

"It's your name, is it not? You've grown, more than anybody would have expected of you and nobody is prouder of your growth than I am. You've shown that even when pushed to the wall, you retain a bulk of your brain power. Your animal instincts reared its head and it would have been simple to give in to it, but you somehow managed to calm down and deduce exactly what I was trying to do. It is why man is a higher animal. Man can process information at a breakneck speed and decide if to follow or to let it go. Most times, the animal nature wants you to pursue and when it senses someone strong or something, it caves into their rule. But the brain refuses to cave in such a way, it fights against animal nature and proves beyond reasonable doubt that there's something stronger, something evolution forgot in the animals. The ability to think coherently and make snappy decisions based on those thoughts. That's what it means to be evolved. You have the brain, you've always had it. But your animal instincts were so suppressed, it was always there. You just needed to be prodded, and shaken up a little. This isn't my usual style but, it sometimes works.

"You're a mad genius." Jacob managed to say, wiping his bloodied lip with the back of his hand. His fist managed to reach Daniel too, after a flurry of misplaced jabs.

"I've heard that before. Shake the world. Little brother. I'll stay out of your hair from now on. Shaking you up has to be my favourite pastime. No hard feelings, eh?" Daniel held out a hand and Jacob stood upright, his back upright.

They struck a little bargain and Daniel walked out of the house without a backward glance. The only problem was… he wasn't sure when his big brother would return, if he ever did. He didn't like to think about it that way but he knew that he'd always be grateful for Daniel, especially when he thought that he was just trying to bring him down for no reason. Correcting that viewpoint, he needed to talk to Sarah: and this time, he was no longer worried.

There was nothing to be worried about.

~~

True to his word, David went to talk to her family. And the resounding no they gave was enough to shake the foundations of the world.

"You think you can just return from God knows where and everything would be just as you left it? No. That isn't how the world works." Listening to Sarah's father, he could see just where she got her mannerisms.

"I know I messed up before and I'm trying to make it right, even though it's technically not easy. I want to do right by her this time, even if it is the last thing I do. I don't want to carry on with mistakes that I made, with things I should have done, words I should have said but I never did. I don't want that, I just don't. And I don't want to feel this choking sensation in the pit of my stomach. I know I've hurt everyone, and I know it's not easy to get forgiveness, so I'll go to the radio and newspaper stations first. I'll return here." He knew that it was probably a lost cause, but he didn't want to just... give up. That was against everything he said to Sarah. Against everything he told her. He didn't want to be the guy who lied to her, didn't want to be the guy who didn't keep a promise. He already had one reputation and it wasn't for anything good. He needed to right the wrongs he did, standing from the ground up.

"It doesn't matter what you do; you won't be accepted into this household again. But carry on, let's see if this would send you scurrying again, with your tails between your legs. That's the one thing I want to see above all. You may leave." Her father said with a tone of finality and David knew that he wasn't going to be able to reach the old man, he just had to try to see if he could reach the others. He owed it to them at the very least. To redeem her name and to stop her from hiding. She disappeared because of him and he didn't know how to feel about it. Did he feel remorseful? Yes. Self-hate? Another yes. And he felt like he was the biggest jerk in the entire solar system, no—the entire universe.

He left her house, his thoughts muddled beyond human comprehension. He wasn't sure where he was to begin, because that article that went viral was posted three years before then. Three whole years. Most people made a few memes off the entire situation and he needed to make them understand that knowing one side of the story was dangerous. He remembered what Sarah told him the day he left.

"Don't just say the truth, that wouldn't endear you to anyone in the public. They love stories of tragic love that somehow reunited. Give them something to talk about for years after today. You have my permission. As long as I know the truth, I don't care what any else knows. If you're

able to pull this off, it can be a little inside joke, known to only those close enough. Don't mess this up."

He wasn't going to dare. He knew that this meant a lot to her, and he wasn't going to botch it with a half-baked story. They needed the sympathy of the world, and for them to overturn the humiliation he placed on Sarah. It was up to him to define how it was going to go and he swore to do his best to make sure that she became a darling of the world once again and she didn't have to hide.

First, he needed something that would shake people out of their slumber, something that would spread by word of mouth even before it officially came out on the papers.

Something that would kickstart a new beginning for him and most of all, for Sarah, and her best friend Renee who stayed with her through the darkest moments of her life, always there, never complaining. He was sure that people like Renee and Daniel didn't exist anymore. They were just the sweetest kind of people ever.

And he was going to do them proud by telling a story that would bring tears even to the eyes of the heartless.

~~

Jacob was the one who called Sarah and asked to meet up and she wondered what was going on. She hadn't given a definite response and she wondered if it was because of that he called her. She went anyway, if only to see what he was going to say. He was her precious friend, no matter what.

"Hello, Sarah. Thanks for coming on such a short notice. That means a lot to me." He said and she smiled, knowing that he was going somewhere. She just wanted him to hit the nail on the head and get it over with.

"I called you here, because I want you to know I respect your decision. I used to think I was in love with you, when all I was doing was projecting. You were exciting and I felt drawn to you. I took that for love. As silly as it sounds, I tried to impress you. Or maybe I tried to impress myself. Because most of the things I did were things I wanted to do for me. For the longest time, I was at a loss for what I was supposed to be, or who I was supposed to be. I'd gotten the fame, the wealth. But I was empty where it mattered, and everybody else but me knew it. I suspect you must have known too. I made excuses for my actions, even if they were nonverbal. I talked about not being able to comprehend emotions, yet I was hurt when you left abruptly. I talked about not being able to understand people, yet I kept looking forward to talking to you, even if we didn't really have anything to talk about. I believe I created an interest in you and somehow, I managed to translate it into something akin to love, as a language. But I don't think I was really in love with you, I think I was just interested in seeing the world through your eyes. Asking you out was my attempt at finding pieces of me. But what I realized was that I put you on the spot without even thinking about how you were feeling, content to let my own feelings override yours. Everything I did, I was projecting my likes into yours. And I'm sorry."

He sounded so sincere, she wanted to hug him like a teddy bear and tell him that everything was going to be alright. But she didn't do that, she did the next best thing.

"I love being your friend and I don't want to ruin that. I don't know if I gave you mixed signals and if I did, I'm sorry. You have to pardon me, I'm learning the ropes, just like you. And I don't have the right to tell you what to feel. I'm sorry I couldn't come clean to you, you're so sweet and special to me, and I didn't want to ruin that. I didn't know how to let you down slowly, or gently. I wanted to tell you, but what was I to say? That I cared about you, but it wasn't in a romantic way? That feels mean to say. I care about you, I won't lie to you. And if you stay, I will do right by you, as a friend." She said, glad to let the weight off her heart. She'd been so worried about it, that she even talked to Renee about her worries.

"I don't think Jacob is that petty. Maybe you're overthinking it because he's your friend. But you need to know that he deserves the truth. Better to hear it from you than to find out later on."

As usual, Renee was spot on. And Sarah said a silent thanks in her heart for Renee coming into her life. So many things took form because of that one single act.

And she'd always be grateful.

~~

“A wedding, huh? Who’d have thought?” Jacob said, sitting across from his brother as they dined together.

“What? Are you jealous?” Daniel teased and he laughed at the ludicrousness of the entire situation.

“Nah, I’m way past that. I’m glad you made me see I was only infatuated with the version of her I thought understood me.” Jacob said, cutting a piece of steak with his fork.

"It's good you realized it because I'll be honest with you. In front of David, you didn't stand a chance. They're what people call star-crossed lovers, they always find each other, no matter how many times they separate. You shouldn't worry about it." Daniel said and Jacob just shook his head, holding back laughter, so he wouldn't choke on the steak he was eating.

"You say the weirdest things." He replied and without missing a beat, Daniel replied, "That's why you're my brother, you're the only one that can tolerate my idiosyncrasies without completely losing it. I suspect I've pushed some people to either depression or madness. Probably one or both." Daniel said, chatting flippantly and Jacob shook his head, knowing that even if he was given the chance to get someone else as a brother, he'd choose Daniel over and over again, even until the end of time.

"Also, I like your secretary. Is she spoken for?" Daniel said out of the blue and Jacob cocked his head to the side to be sure he heard his brother well.

"Who? Diane?" He asked and Daniel said excitedly, "Yes, that's the one. Diane. Such a beautiful name."

He stared at his brother for a while before saying tentatively… "Are you by any chance attracted to Diane?"

"Why, not just attraction, little brother. I suspect I'm in love with her."

If jaws could fall, Jacob's would have reached the floor. He opened his mouth in utter shock, trying to check if he was in the right dimension.

"You're not dreaming, Jacob. Neither are you hallucinating. Diane suits me, don't you think? Been with her a little more than five times and she's like a firecracker. Can't predict what she'd do next. The perfect pair, wouldn't you say?" Daniel kept eating like he hadn't just dropped the biggest bomb straight on Jacob's lap.

"You're insane." Jacob managed to say after a while and Daniel held a thumb up and said, "Yes, that's correct."

And suddenly, he understood that love... was a comet. Sometimes, it was hard to see it coming or even guess where it was going to land. But when it did appear, its impact was felt all over.

But he, he was content with being alone. He was learning to love himself, one step at a time.

~~

The radio and news stations went wild with the story. It was called the story of the decade. The return of a man kidnapped on his wedding day, a man who fought tooth and nail to return to his soulmate. It was on every station, even the ones he never would have expected. They loved the story so much, that they did a weekly feature on it. He began to appear on television, talking about how much he loved Sarah and how sad he was not to attend the wedding they both planned.

The world was turning on its head. And Sarah watched, laughing at the way he'd turn to stare at the camera and say something absolutely cheesy, it'd make her toes curl.

"Every single day, I wondered if I was going to see her again. I prayed to the gods, even the ones I knew not their names. I wanted to find my lady love again. I didn't want her to go with the wind, I wanted her to be with me. It was a lot, and sometimes, I felt delirium cover me like a blanket. And her name is all that was on my lips. I love her and this time... I want to make sure I can love her forever. Because she's everything to me."

The funny thing was that, she knew he wasn't lying about the deliria. All the things he spoke about aside from the kidnapping were true. She could tell he suffered. Every week, he went to her parents to plead for her hand in marriage. And every week, they rejected. He didn't stop, even after the story of Sarah and David was sweeping through the nations. He was a beautiful, beautiful man and he was all hers. She wasn't sure there was anything more fulfilling than that in the world.

"You're positively glowing, you know that right?" Renee said, sitting on the couch with Sarah as they both watched David during an interview.

"I can't help it, he's just so dreamy." Sarah cooed and sighed, staring at the TV. Her mind was way too far gone.

"Yes, that he is." Renee concurred and Sarah was glad that she wasn't the only one seeing it, that someone else could bear witness to it and she wasn't just going crazy and that her man was a total dreamboat.

"He's really fixing everything up. After all these years." Sarah said more to herself than to Renee. She wasn't sure she knew what to feel, or even if there was something to feel. That was how intensely he affected her. Rid her of thoughts and common sense.

"I love him so much, Renee. I love him." She said, holding the hand of her best friend.

“I know you do, sweetheart. I know you do.” Renee said and they shared a conspiratorial smile before they resumed watching David’s interview on the TV.

~~

Diane was waiting for the most amazing man she’d ever seen. And when he popped out a ring, she almost passed out. He was the ultimate find, the one most women would do anything to sink their claws in.

And he was the one person she had no single clue about. She couldn’t read him like she could do to everyone else, he was too unpredictable, and he kept her on her toes. Literally and figuratively. He was energetic in more ways than one. And he made her swoon without even realizing what exactly she was doing. That was the power of love, she at least knew that much.

"Hey love, wanna go out for a bit?" And just as expected, he appeared like the wind, massaging her shoulders. Even with her highly trained senses, she couldn't make sense of how he appeared or when.

"What do you have in mind?" She asked and he gave her a wicked smile, one that was filled with promise.

"I'll go anywhere you take me to." She said at last and he laughed, a loud and cheery laughter, full of mirth and happiness.

Diane was home.

~~

Jacob didn't know how he was supposed to prepare for two weddings when he was hit with the news that Renee's boyfriend just proposed and they were going to wed after Sarah's.

He got an instant headache. His friend, his brother and now, his other friend?

They'd smoothened out their differences when Renee realized he wasn't a threat and there was no need to be wary of him. But now, he had three weddings, and they were all going to wed around the same period.

Thinking about it, he realized that those things weren't for him personally, not while he had a thousand and one things to do. He needed to keep sharp and as long as everybody was happy, that's all that mattered to him. He'd finally accepted himself, especially his quirks and he found it easier to understand people than he'd ever had before. In fact, some would have said he had a weird knack for it. All thanks to Daniel though, because he sure as hell couldn't have done it himself.

But, how the hell was he supposed to prepare for three parties? Was there a sort of manual to it? He could have asked Renee who knew almost everything, if only she wasn't one of those getting married.

At this rate, I'll have grey hair before long. And to think Diane was flirting with me.

His head couldn't take all the information being filtered in at a ridiculous pace. So, he dropped everything and went straight to sleep.

CHAPTER FIFTEEN

Sarah didn't like to give her father a tough time but she decided that he needed it. She'd appeared on various talk shows with David and they were literally the couple sweeping the world away. But her parents were still adamant about her marrying him, so she told them the truth in hopes that they were going to cooperate.

"I'll marry David, with or without your blessings. But I'd prefer if you overlook it this once and give me your blessing." She told her father who stared at her sternly through his medicated glasses.

"Have you forgotten what he did to you? The laughing stock he made of us? What if he does something like that later in the future, what then?" Her father asked and she almost groaned out loud. She was tired of the same back and forth over and over again because no matter how many times she told them that David was trying his best, they didn't listen. Especially her dad. Her mother just kept mum the entire time.

"You preach about forgiveness all the time, Dad. You should practice what you preach, that would do the world a whole lot of good." She said as a parting word and left the house. She was fuming because it was clear that her parents didn't want her to go through that hell again and as sweet as she found it, she also found it stifling. They seemed to forget the fact that she was a fully-fledged adult capable of making her own decisions and every single step she took was to buttress that fact. She was no longer the girl who hid in her father's shadow, she'd become a woman who faced life on her terms and reforged destiny even with her fragile hands. Of course, she had the help of the sisterhood, she didn't need to think about how messed up her life would have been if she didn't have those angels. The thought sent a shiver racing through her spine.

The sisterhood was her safe space, where she could trust to go when she needed to unwind and let things off her chest. No matter who they were, be it spies, assassins, rape survivors, divorcees, etc; they all came together under a common banner, and they chose the kind of life they wanted to live. They reshaped what the world expected of them and did great things, even from small places. They were beyond amazing and whenever she thought of them, tears came to her eyes. They were her people and they'd seen her through the roughest patches of life. They'd stood in solidarity with her when her screams threatened to bring down the sky and her body shook like it was hit by a thousand thunderbolts. They didn't judge or criticize, they listened and that was above all the most beautiful thing anybody had ever done for her. And they did it over and over again, without fail.

There was no Sarah without them and if her parents didn't want to give her their blessing, she was going to go to the very people whose opinion of her mattered more than life itself; her sisterhood.

And this time, she was going to be bold and unashamed.

She survived. That's all that mattered.

~~

"I have something to tell you." Diane said as she lay cuddled in bed with Daniel. It had been bugging her for a while by then and she decided that if she was to get married, she needed to come clean.

“Oh? Hit me.” He said, propping his head on one hand and staring into her eyes. She couldn’t remember being so nervous before. She’d faced death one too many times before and yet, the current prospect in front of her was scarier than any A-ranked mission.

“I’m not who you think I am.” She said and took a deep breath wondering how she was supposed to broach the entire subject. It was opening Pandora’s Box and this time, there was no going back from the consequences.

"Oh? Are you a fairy? A goddess? Or maybe a pony? I always wanted to ride a pony." He said with a small smile on his face and she felt her heart shatter, wondering how she was going to break the news.

"I'm a spy!" She blurted out without thinking and she expected horror, but his facial expression didn't change in the slightest.

"I would have preferred a pony though. But a spy works too." He said and grinned. Her heart hammered in her chest and she wondered if he didn't hear her well.

"Don't look so shell-shocked. You're a spy, yes. Ella Petrikhov. You've been in several covert operations for the Soviet Union before you decided to turn over a new leaf and help the US military instead. The last mission you had was to kill an entire family, including the three children. So, you tipped them off and disappeared off the face of the earth. Considered missing in action and since spies technically don't exist, they erased every trace of you. Is that all?" Daniel said and he was still grinning, not remotely bothered.

"Who are you?" She asked, eyes wide.

"I'm just a guy in love with you. Just a guy. Never forget."

~~

"Are you ever going to tell her?" Brad asked Renee who smiled and said, "No, I don't think so."

"You don't think she deserves to know all you've done for her? Isn't she your best friend?" Brad asked and Renee was contemplative before replying.

"She's not just my best friend, she's my only friend." She said, laying emphasis on the word only.

"So, you won't tell her that you turned down a promotion multiple times and asked to be transferred to a low-ranking station just because of her? You won't tell her you turned down my proposal to marry you more than ten times, just because of her?" Brad seemed to be confused, staring at his fiancée, a quizzical expression on his face.

"There's no point. I love her, and she loves me. She'd do the same for me in a heartbeat, so where's the need?" Renee replied and Brad was at a loss for words.

"I don't think I can ever understand women." He replied at last.

"I don't think you need to." Renee said and smiled sweetly, kissing him on his cheeks before going to where Sarah was.

~~

Jacob heard everything, he was passing and he heard it by chance, but he finally understood what it meant to have a friend. It was putting that friend's need ahead of yours, going the distance and making sure that the friend always stayed on top, even if it meant you'd be below.

He thought he knew of love, of sacrifice. He thought wrong.

He remembered his ex, and how she called him shallow. He could finally understand the extent of her words, listening to Renee and her fiancé. He was always running away from responsibility, telling himself numbers mattered more than anything else, even friendships and relationships. But no matter how much he built businesses, he had no friends, nobody to truly care if he lived or died aside from what they were gaining.

But, he realized that Sarah, Diane, and Renee, were all his friends. True friends this time, not phoney. He didn't need to second guess their actions, he didn't need to convince himself that they were his friends, they just were. And that was what made it worthwhile.

He'd been trying to stand out for the longest time, it was a relief to just... fit in. To not struggle so much to be noticed. Standing apart wasn't as fun as he expected, especially when he finally had people who cared deeply about him.

His antics still made them laugh, but it was all in good faith. He realized that all the while, he'd been bothered about the wrong sort of wealth. Daniel had the right idea, he always did. If he was told that Daniel was clairvoyant, he'd believe it in a heartbeat.

The world was alright, for the first time in a while because he was amongst the coolest people on earth and this time, he intended to have the most fun ever.

Because life was indeed beautiful.

~~

Sarah seeking the acceptance of her sisterhood was funny because they'd accepted her, right from the very beginning. She didn't need to ask for their blessings, they already gave it and they said as much to her.

"You're one of us, whatever comes." Mrs. Dodds said and she kissed the kindly old woman on the cheeks, the old woman who reminded her that life was meant to be lived, to be explored and not just in confines. Life had different forms across the ages and sometimes most people didn't realize when life was staring at them right in the face. They hunt after what life means, forgetting life is all about this moment and nothing else. The moment that extends into an eternity.

"Our blessing? Or rather, we need yours." Diane said and the others laughed. Renee was the next to speak and Sarah waited with bated breath.

"As many times as you need my blessing, I'll give it. Even if it's close to infinity."

Renee spoke with sincerity and Sarah burst into tears. She couldn't hold it back anymore and who could blame her? She had the most formidable forces of women in the world, women who weren't afraid to wear their hearts on their sleeves, women who weren't afraid to stare into the unknown and create art. She had women who stared death in the face and laughed, women whom death was wary of.

She was protected across all fronts, she was safe.

~~

After realizing that their opinions didn't count, her parents caved in and gave their blessing even though she didn't need it anymore by then, but she accepted it in good faith. She knew they were worried about her and stuff, but she also wanted him to know that with her sisterhood, messing with her was synonymous with death. They were important to her, more so than most people.

"Hello, Sarai." And suddenly, the world fell out of its axis. At that moment, only two people remained, Sarah and David.

"You say my name like it's a worship." She said, shivering slightly and he came close, close enough to whisper into her ears.

"You're my religion. Now and forever."

She'd heard cheesy words before, but whenever David spoke, she found out that she needed to catch her breath. He did things to her that most people would have likened to voodoo, especially the way his voice washed over her like wine down her throat.

She could see only him, he was all that existed to her, and everybody else was taking second place. She didn't even bother trying to look around, that wasn't her home. Her home with David and it would always be.

"Dear Sarai... may I have this dance?" He bowed so smoothly, that her breath caught in her throat. And when her eyes met his... the entire universe came undone. There was a clashing of constellations as stars were thrown out of orbit and the world was reformed right in his eyes.

"You may," she tried to say but her voice came out husky and he took her hand. When they moved, she could feel moments slipping away, losing form, and tumbling into the void. They were all that mattered, and the world could burn for all she cared. She couldn't imagine being with anybody else but the beautiful man in front of her.

He was her fantasy-made flesh, her reality.

All hers. And she wasn't going to share, not with anyone. Not even for all the treasures in the world.

~~

"So, how do you feel?" Jacob asked Sarah as they danced and he could see her practically glowing, especially after the dance she had with David.

"I feel like I'm untouchable. Like nothing can hurt me. Is that hubris?" She asked and he didn't need to think of a reply because there was one right there, staring at them.

"You are untouchable, don't ever doubt that." He said and she smiled at him. A smile of friendship.

"Would you like to be a godfather?" She asked him out of the blue and he was taken aback but he managed to get himself in time.

"I'd love to. You know that." He said, beside himself with joy. He was wondering if someone would ask him and he was glad that Sarah beat everyone else to the punch.

"Thank you, Jacob. For being here." She said and he knew that his presence meant a lot to her, deep down.

"I don't think I'd rather be anywhere else. Today, one of my closest friends in the world is getting married. And I'm there to see it. Also, to eat the food, don't forget the food." He quipped and she laughed out loud saying, "Daniel must be rubbing off on you and he turned to look at his brother, realizing that it was true.

"I suppose he has."

CHAPTER SIXTEEN

It's been one whole year since the weddings that shook the world. Three weddings in succession, three close friends. It was practically the stuff books were made of. Jacob had finally decided to further his studies, deciding that a PhD would be an excellent way to while away time. He loved the world of research and said as much to Sarah whenever he sent a mail.

Sarah had given birth to a beautiful child by then. He was two months old and a hell-raiser, much like his father.

"You think he'd be a charmer when he grows up?" David asked her, and she rolled her eyes as though he was asking a pretty obvious question. Which, in retrospect, he was.

“Of course. I hope he doesn’t charm a poor lady off her feet and make her take leave of her senses.” Sarah said, and David wiggled his brows as though he knew what she was talking about. “And who might this reference be about? Maybe my best friend, Daniel? He’s one guy I still haven’t figured out yet.” David said, and Sarah shook her head. She knew he was deliberately acting obtuse, which was one reason she loved him: they could play and have fun like children, with none being the wiser.

"You know it's you." She said, jostling his shoulder, and he looked at her in mock surprise, exclaiming, "Me? You stole my heart right out of my chest you little fire devil." He quipped, making mention of her hair. He had a different nickname every time so she didn't bother trying to keep track of them all.

"Oh and, Jacob's letter arrived this morning. Do me the honour of reading it out loud while I take care of the baby?" She asked but it wasn't really a question, it was a command and he knew better than to protest about it.

Dear Sandersons,

I quite like Asia. There's something mystically charming about the entire continent, it's as though it's far removed from the modern world and yet ingrained in it somehow. To call it a womener would be an understatement. I've decided to go to Australia next, since I have a newfound fascination for animals bigger than I am. How's little Moses? Wonder why you two went with that name, he was a lot more trouble in the Bible, unless I am reading it all wrong.

I think that the world needs more of little babies like Moses and I'll do my best to ensure that before I return, I'll find a woman much to my liking. And maybe I can finally get married and leave the single lifestyle. The sea is not so bad, if you're a fan of monotony. I find out it helps me think, the endless stretch of water as far as the eyes can see. Even binoculars. It makes me appreciate just how massive this world is, if one sea can wow me so. I've taken it upon myself to check out the seven seas of the world, probably at a later date because my research sends me far and wide into the world.

Sometimes I don't know if I'm coming or I'm going. I suspect that I'll find what I've been looking for, or maybe I hope I'll find it. Soon. I should be making my way back as soon as I do. Tell Moses that his godfather will be back soon. I hope he recognizes my voice (from the womb, that is). Take care of yourselves and be the best version of yourselves you can be.

Yours surreptitiously,

(I like using words to confuse you, Sarah)

"He's still a child, I see." Sarah remarked as she tried to get little Moses into a diaper. "We're all children at heart, my love." David said and Sarah then realized he wasn't doing anything.

"Good, then you'd be able to communicate more with Moses. Make sure his diapers are done properly." She said and handed him the baby. He shook his head and laughed.

She was the most beautiful woman existence had ever conjured up.

It'd been one full year since Daniel and Diane got married and they seemed to be more in love each day than the last. One would think they married the day before.

"You still haven't told me how you were able to get into my safe box and take the present meant to be a surprise for you." Diane said in mock indignation and Daniel laughed heartily. He usually played harmless pranks on her just for the fun of it.

"A magician never reveals his secrets," he said and she rolled her eyes. He was a master at everything, and even she who'd been through some pretty messed up things and had to adapt found it hard to keep up with him. Daniel was just on a different level entirely, she still couldn't comprehend it. They'd decided to hold off on the children because they needed to spend more time together and it was working beautifully for them.

"Do you know how much I love you?" She asked him and he held up four fingers. He was so silly, she couldn't help the grin that morphed onto her face.

"No, silly. How can you say four? Four what? Million? Thousand?

Billion?" She asked and yet he still held up four fingers.

"Just four?" She said, staring at him in mock surprise. He shouldn't have surprised her but he always did, whether she liked it or not.

"Oh you, I'll get you for this." She said and tried to run after him but he evaded and reclined on the wall as though he had nothing better to be doing.

"You're so infuriating." She said, balling her fingers into fists.

"And you're so in love with me. Admit it." He said and she replied, "But I just did!"

"Oh, you did? Maybe I didn't hear you. Can you say it again?" He wasn't done talking before she threw her slippers at him. "It's comfortable here, isn't it?" Brad asked Renee, staring at her bulging stomach. He couldn't for the life of him figure out why she wanted a child so early.

"Yes, it is." She said and seeing her just lie there, it tugged at his heartstrings. They put off the world tour until their baby was around two years old.

"Do you miss your friends?" He asked her out of the blue, wondering if staying so far away from the others was a good idea.

"Not really. I have the internet. It's not like we're cavemen or in this case, cavewomen." He was tempted to agree, although he still worried, because the bond they shared wasn't just surface level, at all. It was something else entirely, something new and unexplored. They were at home with themselves and he couldn't remember seeing anything more wholesome than that in his life.

"I know, I know. I just worry sometimes." He said and she shook her head, and motioned for him to come closer.

"They once had me for a ridiculously long time, and now you have me. For as long as you want. Or, are you tired of me?" She said with a pouty expression and he knew there and then that he'd move mountains, upturn streams, turn the world to a barren wasteland, whatever was required for the smile on her face to never falter.

"I can't ever get tired of you, Amor. You're my life. And I've waited every day for years, waiting for when you'd be mine. I love you beyond the confines of this world and I'll prove it time and time again, as many times as required. You're all I need, all I want." He said and she smiled.

"Overzealous much?" She asked, a wicked glint in her eyes. He was in love with the woman in front of him, she'd consumed his senses and made nonsense of his inhibitions. She made him want to scream from the rooftops, to scream her name for the entire world to hear.

"For you; always. What do you think we should call the baby?" He asked her and they started to think.

"If it's a boy, I'd like him to be called Jay, from Jacob. If it's a girl, Sai, from Sarah."

He knew that was the final word on it. If Renee had something on her mind, nothing could dissuade her, nothing in all the earth.

"I know you must be wondering. I guess I got to understand Jacob and how being different wasn't a curse, it was sometimes a blessing. And Sarah, I took care of her, because I loved her from the depths of my soul. And she returned that love in equal measure, not taking a break even for a single day. She was there for me, and I was there for her. Together, we were able to create something out of nothing." He loved listening to Renee, even while pregnant, she seemed to shine like a thousand suns. She was glowing and he wondered if there was anybody else that could compare to her majesty.

Probably not.

“Will you tell them you’ve chosen those names?” He asked her and she said a vehement no.

“When they find out, I want it to be of their own accord. Maybe when the baby is born. They are both different phases of my life, phases that I couldn’t have survived without. I’m here with you, because of them. I owe them this much at the very least.

“I understand, Amor. I completely understand.” He said, rubbing her stomach as she purred in delight and satisfaction. He was sweating buckets, sweat dripping into his eyes as Renee was wheeled into the labour room, and he followed after, wearing a surgical gown, gloves and face mask. He knew that when the child was coming into the world, he wanted his face to be the very first one it saw.

He wanted to be the father in both words and deeds. Renee wasn't screaming like most of the movies he'd watched, she was taking deep breaths and he was even more frazzled than she was.

"I'm here, I'm not leaving your side." He said, taking her hand in his as a show of reassurance. She squeezed once and twice before the pangs of labour began.

He was confused, he didn't know what to do or if anything he intended to do was going to help. To say he was shaken was an understatement of the century.

"I'm not leaving your side love, not even for a single second. Listen to my voice, don't be shaken. I'm here."

"Hold me." She said and he did, especially when the doctors asked her to push. Brad remembered the feeling of fear wrapping itself around him, as a tear dropped from the eye of one of the strongest women he'd ever seen.

"Don't fret, my love. Hold my hand. I'm here for you." He kept speaking even though he wasn't sure that he was listening to him anymore. He didn't stop, he started telling her about the first time they met. And how they met Sarah. He told her how the university was and how most people they jointly knew thought they were a weird couple. He told her how weird it was when Sarah began to follow her around. He kept talking, not keeping track of what he was saying, he just knew that she needed to hear his voice, she needed proof that he was still with her. And he'd give her all the proof she needed in the world, he wasn't going to hold back even for a single second.

"I loved you then, I love you even more now. I can't imagine living, not knowing you're by my side. I'll say these words to you when we're old and grey and when the world takes on a different shade. I'll remind you of how far we've come, the battles we've fought. You've been there through thick and thin, through things I wouldn't have survived alone. You're strong enough for both of us. And you don't flaunt your strength, it's just a part of you. Your emotional strength, your physical strength, your wisdom, your love, your care, your attention to detail." He paused, hoping that he wasn't rambling but deciding to continue anyway because his wife needed his voice.

"Do you remember when a lecturer sent for you and the students in the class gave way at once? It was as though you were a goddess and they always parted ways whenever you walked past. You were a hurricane, my love. You were someone I knew even back then that you'd redefine my existence. And you have, Amor. You have. In so many ways, you've made me attuned to the emotions of others, and you've taught me not to judge so harshly. You've been there for me when I was at my lowest and you thought nothing of it. You didn't make fun of me or make me feel lower than I was. Instead, you listened. I can't forget how you claimed to hate toast yet you ate it because I was sick and you wanted to show me that the toast was alright. You saved me when I was failing and put me through the things I couldn't understand. You made it easy for me and you did it so effortlessly. You reached out to me even when you didn't have to and made me feel safer than I've ever felt in my life. You've sacrificed so much for me and I don't think anybody else can ever compare."

And then the cry of a baby rents the air. As he was about to jubilate, he heard another baby's cry.

His wife had given birth to twins.

You said it, Amor. You said it. And you did it. Sai and Jay are in this world because of you. Because of you, love. I love you so much. I can't explain it because there are no words. You're here, and they're here. The family is complete." He said, trying to hold back tears, but he couldn't. Tears ran freely down his face. “Don’t cry. We’re all here.” Renee said. Though her voice was weak, and for as long as he lived. He knew that he wouldn’t ever forget the sound of her voice. On that day. The vulnerability, the softness. "Yes, Amor. I won’t cry. I’m just so happy.” He said, repeatedly kissing the back of her hand and knowing their bond lived on in his children. Amor smiled, tears glistening in her own eyes. She had always dreamed of this moment, of being surrounded by her loved ones and knowing that they were all safe and together. Even though she knew her time was limited, she felt at peace knowing that Renee would continue to protect and guide Sai and Jay.

As the family sat silently, enjoying each other's presence, Renee's voice suddenly broke through the peaceful atmosphere. "We must prepare for battle," she said firmly.

Everyone turned to look at her, confusion evident on their faces. "What do you mean?" Amor asked worriedly.

"I have seen it in my visions," Renee replied. "Darkness is coming.

A great evil is rising once again, and we must be ready to fight." Sai and Jay looked at each other nervously, knowing they would play an essential role in this upcoming battle. Amor could feel the tension building in the room as everyone silently prepared themselves for what would come.

But despite the fear in their hearts, there was also a sense of determination and unity among them. They were a family now, brought together by love and fate. And they would face whatever challenge came their way together.

Renee led them into the training grounds, where they spent hours honing their skills with sword fighting and magic until sweat dripped from their brows and exhaustion set in. But even then, none wanted to stop - they were too determined to be ready when darkness finally arrived.

As night fell over the kingdom, Amor stood atop a tower overlooking the land with Sai and Jay by her side. In the distance, a storm was brewing - literally and figuratively - as dark clouds gathered overhead.

"We will face this together," Amor said confidently as she held her hand for them to take.

Sai took one hand while Jay took the other, their bond stronger than ever before. And as they watched the storm approach, they knew that no matter what happened, they would always be a family. A family forged by love and ready to face any challenge that came their way. Together, they stood tall and prepared for battle. Because in this world filled with darkness, there was always a glimmer of light - the love of a family that would never be broken.

THE END

THE REJECTION

Printed in Great Britain
by Amazon